GARGOYLES

GARGOYLES

stories

BILL GASTON

ANANSI

First published in hardcover in 2006 by House of Anansi Press Inc.

This edition published in 2007 by
House of Anansi Press Inc.
110 Spadina Avenue, Suite 801
Toronto, ON, M5V 2K4
Tel. 416-363-4343
Fax 416-363-1017
www.anansi.ca

Distributed in Canada by
HarperCollins Canada Ltd.
1995 Markham Road
Scarborough, ON, M1B 5M8
Toll free tel. 1-800-387-0117

Distributed in the United States by
Publishers Group West
1700 Fourth Street
Berkeley, CA 94710
Toll free tel. 1-800-788-3123

House of Anansi Press is committed to protecting our natural environment. As part of our efforts, this book is printed on Rolland Enviro paper: it contains 100% post-consumer recycled fibres, is acid-free, and is processed chlorine-free.

11 10 09 08 07   1 2 3 4 5

LIBRARY AND ARCHIVES CANADA CATALOGUING IN PUBLICATION

Gaston, Bill, 1953–
        Gargoyles : stories / Bill Gaston.

ISBN-13: 978-0-88784-749-3 (bound). — ISBN-10: 0-88784-749-8 (bound).
ISBN-13: 978-0-88784-776-9 (pbk.) — ISBN-10: 0-88784-776-5 (pbk.)

1. Gargoyles — Fiction.   I. Title.

PS8563.A76G37 2006   C813'.54   C2006-902827-3

Library of Congress Control Number: 2007927970

Cover design: Bill Douglas at The Bang
Text design and typesetting: Sari Naworynski
Author photograph: Clownbog Studios

Canada Council   Conseil des Arts
for the Arts   du Canada

ONTARIO ARTS COUNCIL
CONSEIL DES ARTS DE L'ONTARIO

We acknowledge for their financial support of our publishing program the Canada Council for the Arts, the Ontario Arts Council, and the Government of Canada through the Book Publishing Industry Development Program (BPIDP).

Printed and bound in Canada

For Dede Crane

CONTENTS

Wrathful

THE NIGHT WINDOW

Tyler's librarian mother has brought home two for him. He hefts them, drops them onto his bed. One is on fly fishing. The second is *Crime and Punishment*. Tyler suspects Dostoevsky is a writer he will read only if made to — for instance, if it's the only book he brings on this camping trip.

Tyler knows that what he is actually weighing here is his degree of insubordination. Yesterday his mother's boyfriend — Kim — went through all their gear, inspecting wool sweaters and cans of food. Peering into Tyler's hardware store plastic bag he shook his head and pointed in at the new reading-light with its giant dry cell battery.

"It's a natural-light camping trip," he said, unpointing his finger to waggle it, naughty-naughty, in Tyler's face. Tyler saw how he could fall to an easy hate of his mother's boyfriend, except that Kim was just always trying to be funny. His mother had explained this early on.

"Umm . . . no lights?" his mother began, half-coming to Tyler's defence. "If I have to pee in the middle of the night? Kim, you want some *on* you?"

It was this kind of statement (which had Kim laughing overloud) that made Tyler turn away blank-faced, that made him not want to go camping, and let his mother go wherever she wanted without him. It must be exactly this sort of statement that offends her co-workers at the library; it's the reason she fits nowhere, and dates someone like Kim Lynch.

Natural light. Why, he thinks, plucking up the Dostoevsky, should he take orders from Kim Lynch anyway? Kim has red hair and see-through skin, is short and muscular — even his round face acts like a muscle. Tyler's mother is at least an inch taller, and so thin that Tyler knows he will be thin for life too. And: "Kim." His mother should reconsider on grounds of name alone. Tyler secretly agrees with him on this business of natural light, how its spirit probably goes with the quiet of flyfishing. But Tyler doesn't want to take orders. If there's one thing he's learned about his mother it's that no one that age — no one — knows what's going on and everything is up for grabs. At first this depressed him, then not. Like in the animal world, it's a big jungle-mix of hunger and wits and power. Accepting this is the difference between turning adult and remaining a child, which is how he explained it to his mother a month ago. She listened attentively, relishing his braininess and such, then rose from her kitchen chair, patted his shoulder, said, "I have been released from my duties as a mother," and left the room. His mother tries to be funny much of the time too.

Tyler tries to read Dostoevsky during the drive, which is three hours north then an hour west on gravel to a lake. Kim's SUV is not as roomy as one is led to believe from the street, where its design suggests shoulders and size. Tyler is forced to listen to Kim being forced to listen to his mother's harangue about SUVs polluting twice as much as transportation needs to and how their owners never drive them up impossible mountains like they do in every ad on TV. Kim is sweetly pleased for he gets to say, "The word is 'off-road.' That is what we're doing — we're *going* 'off-road.'" But Tyler mostly agrees with her. It's wrong to contaminate fly-fishing with an SUV. Fly-fishers should walk.

In any case reading is difficult three feet from his mother and her new sexual partner. He has seen Kim, even while driving, glance down at her breasts. This morning, loading the car, when they thought Tyler wasn't looking they performed a quick leering pantomime of zipping two sleeping bags together. Even their discussions of which gas station or favourite chocolate bar or how much sugar in the diet or is beer the same kind of sugar or are the Republicans trying to take over the world or blindly receiving it by default — here in the SUV all of his mother's lilts of voice sound to Tyler like minor variations on one basic sexual position. All this veiled eagerness makes him want to be home alone.

Why is he here? Mothers don't go camping with relatively new boyfriends and ask the sixteen-year-old son along. Tyler sees that she doesn't love Kim all that much, not in the way he's seen her with other boyfriends, she as obvious as a puppy panting over doggy-dish dreams of a nice nuclear family. He has seen her want some men that badly, where eventually she takes the deep hopeful breath and offers Tyler up as part of the package, hauling him out like an extra 130-pound arm she's been hiding behind her back. It isn't like that with Kim, though. So what is this about? Why is he along?

It seems that his mother has decided to be his friend. And that she sees this trip to be exactly this: Three friends, going camping. Tyler wonders if anything could be more naive.

"Tyler? Here it is. It's right around this long bend."

"Here what is?" Tyler takes his face out of the book. She's talking to him and he's finally been pulled in by Dostoevsky, whom he has decided is basically an entertaining neurotic. Taken a step further it would be paranoid comedy.

"The giant elf! The twenty-foot face! The one that really freaks me out!"

They round a bend and Tyler keeps his head out of Russian neuroses long enough to see that whatever it is his mother wants him to see is gone. She pretends to wail like a child. Kim knew of the statue too and recalls now that it was removed because of cars slowing to look at it and causing accidents.

His mother turns to Tyler. "He had this giant pointy hat. One arm pointed right at you, there in your car, and the other pointed at their driveway. It was a go-cart place or something. But the thing was forty feet tall! It was totally unnecessary and really, really ugly. I mean it was all face! It was like —"

"It was really stupid-looking," Kim affirms.

"— It was like some kid made it out of papier mâché. It used to really freak me out." She gives Kim a look. "When I was Tyler's age, it used to *really* freak me out."

His mother means drugs. Kim gives her a sly smile back, as though he *really* understands. Tyler can tell he *really* doesn't.

It's maybe the main thing he hates about his mother, how everyone she meets has to be informed what an extreme hippy she was. Tyler has several times been with his mother and one of her old friends and they'll see some rainbow-clad extrovert skip past in bare feet with bubbles drifting from her dreadlocks or something, and Tyler will snort, and the friend will say, Well, you should have seen your *mother* back then. At this his mother laughs and revels as if the sun is on her face.

His mother doesn't have many friends left from "back then." Tyler thinks they avoid her. He's told her about it, how "back then" looks like the only thing that was ever important to her and she can't shut up about it. Even the *way* she can't shut up about it. Sometimes she says "back in the daze," pronouncing it with a grimace so the spelling is understood and implies how much she used to get stoned. And Tyler will watch the friend answer with that first nervous stoned-memory smile and then it's all smiling one-upmanship, competing little stories about seeing personality in foliage, etc.

One thing in particular that his mother says sickens him. If someone asks her where she came from, her answer, "I came in through the bathroom window," Tyler knows was in a Beatles song. It makes him shrink and wince. He's heard her say it at least twice. It sums up what's worst in her, how she makes like there's this huge mystery to her when it's clear to him and everyone else that there's no mystery at all. None. Where she's really from is Vancouver. She pronounces it Van*kew*ver.

What Tyler figures is that she never really was a hippy. Real hippies were too damaged to read. She went to university, she's a librarian with staff under her. Now, when people see her coming, with that old-fashioned smile on her face, they see a librarian who's still trying to be someone she never was.

After Campbell River they leave the highway to drive smaller and smaller logging roads, then reach a clearing beside a lake. A homemade picnic table marks it as a place to camp. They set up two tents about ten feet apart, and throw sleeping bags into each. When they're done, Tyler's mother points and says, "Hey, not fair. Tyler has a tent all to himself," and Kim gamely smiles and pretends to be annoyed at this too.

Leaving his mother to sort through the food, Kim takes Tyler off to fly-fish. Tyler has spincast for trout before and he's fair at it. Though he lacks biceps he has strength when needed. Kim leads him along a path for maybe a hundred yards, saying nothing except the curious, "Not a lot of birds, eh?"

They emerge into another clearing at a small gravel beach. Tyler is disappointed to see another picnic table. This isn't quite the wilderness spot he assumed. Searching the ground he notes the telltale curls of old line and the faded neon card-board of fishing lure packs. Kim places the gear on the table and begins assembling the rods.

"These are cane," he explains. "They're the real thing."

"Great," Tyler says.

"We'll try a nymph replica on yours, and I'll start with a . . . with an alien express."

"Sounds good." He hears what he thinks is an owl, but knows it might be a dove, and doesn't want to ask.

"So this is your first time, right?"

"Yes."

"There's no such thing as an 'alien express.' Made that one up."

"Ah. Right."

Kim laughs, possibly because Tyler doesn't.

"I should have caught that," Tyler says. "Didn't sound much like a fly."

"Gotta watch me, Tyler, I'm fast."

"I'll try."

Kim pulls off his long-sleeved shirt and they take their rods and wade into the lake on a finger of gravel. It's extremely cold, but since Kim seems not to notice, Tyler is careful to step bravely. Kim begins to cast, describing the basic movements. The wrist, he explains, stays stiff. When he first learned, he says, he let his wrist "get into the game too much," and it made the line whip and the fly snapped right off. "It landed right beside my leg."

Tyler doesn't like the sight of his mother's boyfriend's body. It's compact, what you'd almost call little except that he has overt muscles and he wears a tight sleeveless shirt — well, a tank top — to show it all off. Plus on one shoulder a tattoo that reads "Digger." Plus he has no grace. Casting, his arms look too short and his neck stiffens and he lurches like he's throwing boulders at something he's mad at. Reddish hairs drift out from under the muscle-shirt straps on his back.

Tyler tries a few casts. He can see he would improve if he ever spent the time. The breeze, though, stymies him while it doesn't appear to affect Kim's casts at all. But this breeze means no mosquitoes. All in all it's a beautiful day. Tyler can see one snow-capped peak to the west.

"What's 'digger' refer to?"

"Old friend." Kim's tone is the badly acted tragic one that says, I don't want to talk about it. But he adds, "We were in the military."

"You were in the military?"

"I grew up in the Maritimes, gimme a break," Kim says, and then laughs loudly.

And now Kim has hooked a trout. His face deadens and he is serious. It's the first time Tyler has seen him like this, all business. You would swear he's angry.

Over the next hour or so, Kim catches three more rainbows, which he deposits in the nest of ferns in his creel. Finally Tyler hooks one. It's fun to play; it's almost shocking on this thin rod. The fish looks maybe a foot long, exactly the same size as Kim's, and as it splashes around Tyler's knees Kim suggests they release it.

"Why?" asks Tyler. He's horrified Kim will claim that this one's too small, which would reveal far too much about the man his mother likes.

"Well, we have enough. Your mom brought that chili for tonight. All we need's a little side dish."

Tyler watches Kim gently unhook the trout with the needle-nose pliers he wears Velcroed to his leg, his motions so expert that Tyler understands that of course Kim would know exactly how much trout everyone would want with chili. But Tyler sort of wanted to keep his trout and Kim should have asked him. Also, he doesn't like to discover that, already having enough fish to eat, they'd simply been casting until Tyler caught one. He hates it that Kim has been waiting patiently for the unlucky dim-wit.

At the campsite his mother exclaims about the trout, which Kim has laid out on some fresher ferns. All agree how plump and bright and perfect they look.

"He got a few and I got a few," Kim lies with no prompting and without looking at Tyler, as if he's committing some kind of golden self-sacrifice.

"He got four and I got one," says Tyler.

"We had a good time," Kim offers.

Tyler's mother murmurs something about their wide open eyes, about their expressions not changing even when you kill them.

"Can you have a beer, there, Tyler?" Kim asks him in a stage voice, even cupping his hand to one side of his mouth. Winking as if to say, *You can have a beer no matter what your mother says*, he pops the rings of two cans and places them on the table. Then he removes a fish-knife from a sheath on his belt along with a sharpening stone from its own little case also on the belt.

Tyler is still angry with Kim but has said nothing, preferring instead simply not to speak to him at all. On the path back to camp Kim had shouted "Cougar!" and scared the hell out of him. It was such an easy juvenile prank that it wasn't funny at all, despite Kim's minute of laughter and pointing. Tyler is dreading tonight. How long can you sit around a campfire with your mother and a man named Kim Lynch?

"He can have one beer," his mother says, just as overloud, though she is serious.

Something in him wishes she had said no to the beer. But mostly Tyler wonders if anyone besides him is aware of the absurdity of this discussion at all, how since he turned fifteen his mother, convinced of his social awkwardness, encouraged him to "have a couple and relax" at any of the infrequent parties he went to, whether there would be alcohol there or not. In any case he has had his share of beer; once he had two plus a shot of rum.

"I don't want one," Tyler says. He has turned his back on the opened beer can and is about to add that beer doesn't seem to go with the art of fly-fishing, but then Kim would have to respond to this, and Tyler doesn't want him to talk.

It's by far the worst thing his mother has ever said. They are sitting around the picnic table, finished with chili and trout, which was excellent together, and they are quite jolly. Tyler has silently gone to the cooler himself, twice, and he is finishing his second beer. His mother and Kim have had more than that. They have been trading repulsive romantic glances and such for a few minutes now, and then she says it.

"Time for you to take a little walk, Tyler."

His mother looks at him like a buddy. She might as well have thrown him a shitty wink. Tyler is so tight in the stomach that he can't talk.

He goes to his tent for a few deep breaths and a sweater. Maybe socks and runners instead of these sandals. No. Maybe the Dostoevsky. No. With a foot he kicks his pillow and is surprised by what is under it. He stoops. Still in the hardware store bag, his forbidden reading light. His mother has smuggled it along and hidden it here for him.

Emerging from his tent, deliberately not doing up the bug zipper, he sees Kim at the picnic table, red-faced, stiffly repositioning the clean dishes, his pinched and painful smile.

Tyler hates only his mother who, not looking at him, hums a tuneless song. Tyler walks past her, close, hitting her hair with his elbow. He bends at the cooler and grabs three cans of beer. Two he stuffs in his pockets and the other he pops open.

"Tyler could go fishing," Kim says helpfully to the dishes.

Tyler tilts the beer can back as he walks away. He doesn't know why he does it, but he pats Kim's SUV on what would have been its fat ass.

Aside from the one to the fishing spot there are no real paths, so Tyler strikes out along the vehicle track that will eventually reach the logging road. This narrow track is only two ruts for tires, with stiff grass and shrubs growing two feet high in the middle, which, as they drove in, loudly brushed the underbelly of the SUV, making Kim close his eyes and hiss, "Yes, there! *Ohh* yes!" and so on, wriggling in his seat as if this was where all the scratching was taking place.

Walking, sipping beer, Tyler decides that slapping the SUV is exactly something his father would have done. He has never met his father, and hardly thinks of him — well, how can he? — except when he does something slightly surprising. Grabbing these beer was the father-in-him too. When Tyler used to bring up the subject of his father, his mother wouldn't speak of him except in the vaguest generalities — he was unstable, he was too serious, he was very thin. It was this suspicious lack of detail plus a certain stricken look in her eye that told him his mother possibly wasn't sure who his father was. So Tyler stopped asking. In fact, not asking is exactly how his father would have handled it. Sometimes, when Tyler is this angry at his mother, like now, he imagines this is how his father felt about her too and is why he didn't stay.

The forest is dense and the sunset's light is more dark than dappled. The road is narrow and not ditched and the trees are close — if he walks like an arms-out Jesus, Jesus with a beer can in each hand, Tyler can almost touch leaves on either side. He likes the idea, the threat, of a predator. A predator keeps you alert. The lack of man-eating predators in England is partly what's wrong with the overall character of the English, a favourite author of his wrote. Getting attacked is less likely than getting hit by lightning, but truly there are bears and cougars here, perhaps twenty feet away, watching him walk. As far as cougars go, he knows not to make quick or skittery movements. In other words, don't act like prey. In the same way that, sleeping in a new bedroom in another artsy old house they've rented, he sometimes dreads yet wants to see a ghost, he now half-wills a mountain lion to make itself known to him. He would love to see its calm face.

Tyler reaches another logging road and turns left, which is uphill and not the way they had come. He wants to see what lies beyond. He walks and walks. He thinks of nothing he's left behind him. For a while, he visualizes himself very tall, which changes the road's gravel to huge boulders, and he is a Tree Ent, his strides huge and ungainly, his style of walking not just mind over matter but wisdom over matter. As another beer can empties, he places it upright in full view at the side of the road.

He hasn't cried and he won't. He knows he's really all she has in her life. He has just realized that she truly doesn't know what will hurt him. That's how naive and trusting she is — she thinks he is that mature, that above it all. That's how stupid she is — she thinks he is that smart.

He's a few miles from Kim's ass-tickling road when he turns another corner and there, with a driveway of sorts leading to it, is a log cabin. The cabin's roof is so thick with moss that at first Tyler sees it as thatch, the quaintly rounded English kind. Behind the house a shed of equal size looks ready to collapse in on itself. The wood of both buildings is unpainted, perhaps never-painted. There is no car. No lights are on. Tyler sees no electric wires leading to the house, then remembers he has been walking for miles without seeing power poles at all.

Tyler looks around him, sees only trees and hears only the wind in trees higher up the slope. No cars passed him all evening. He really is very alone here. He is in no danger whatsoever so there is no reason to be afraid of anything at all. He has had five cans of beer. He doesn't bother to walk quietly as he approaches the cabin. Why should he? He walks up, cups his hands over his eyes, leans against the glass to look.

On open shelves sit colourful rows of canned goods, and boxes of herbal tea and tins of this and that. A good, or at least big, stereo system sits in the corner. He sees electric light fixtures. Maybe there's a generator in the shed. Tyler wonders if there's indoor plumbing. He will look in other windows. Passing the door he puts his hand on the knob and it turns. Why not? His father would look around too. He is one step inside when he hears . . . The black pickup is new and quiet enough to have been muffled by wind in the treetops and by Tyler's criminal excitement. It rolls up and turns into the head of the driveway before Tyler can move. He can hear shouts inside the truck even before the passenger door opens and a second later, though the truck is still moving, the driver's side opens too.

Tyler is running. No decision, he is instantly behind the house and into the trees. Maybe one of them looked a little fat. Maybe he saw tattoos, maybe he didn't, but they are the type. One shouts a single *Hey*, that's all, and he wishes they were shouting at him from a distance but God he can hear the crunching twigs and the grunts not far behind him.

He's well into the bush now. He has been stabbed in the ribs by a broken branch and yelled because of it. He has tripped twice but is hardly on the ground before he is full speed again. He's not sure his father ran. He leaps a small creek and, absurdly, seeing a hint of depth wonders if it might hold small trout. He lands beside a pale skunk cabbage and smells its garbage smell. He hesitates long enough to hear the crashings behind him. Maybe they are more distant. *No*, he hears crashing to his right now too. Tyler goes left, dodging trees, plunging through vines, more trees, saplings caught under his armpits and scraping them. He sees the light of a clearing and heads for it — maybe he's faster than them on open ground. He hears the men shouting at each other or maybe at him. He plunges into the light of the clearing and he instantly goes down choking as a ghost gets him sharp by the neck and ankles both.

Tyler lies thrashing, unable to breathe. He doesn't think he's dying. He can breathe a little now, and a little more. The low sun is in his eyes. He doesn't care about the men any more, though he hears them coming, walking now, crunching under-brush, breathing hard.

"He went right through the deer fence," one says.

"He *broke* the deer fence," the other adds.

"Did he get a shock?"

"I don't know."

"Hey," one of them asks, louder, almost on him now, "did you get a shock?" The voice sounds concerned but also just curious.

Two pairs of legs are at his head. Tyler manages to sit up. He rubs his throat and coughs. No one touches him.

"What the fuck, man?" one of them asks, and Tyler looks into the setting sun.

The other voice laughs insincerely and says, "Well, I guess he found it."

Both men, standing over Tyler, catching their breath like him, seem mostly nervous now.

The generator is down so they sit in the soft light of strategi-cally placed candles. "Welcome to black mass," one of them, the ponytailed one, said as he began lighting them. Tyler is no longer afraid. He is used to this one's humour — on the walk back he joked about both *Deliverance* and cannibalism — all supposed to put Tyler at ease, he could see that. He also joked about Tyler being the skinniest cop they'd ever seen. Early on they told him their names, which Tyler only half-heard. The ponytail one was Bob, Ben, Burt, something, and the other's was longer. When talking to each other they didn't use names. They seemed very close.

The non-ponytailed one is almost fat and has long hair too, and a moustache, an old-fashioned, biker kind. Both men wear really good sneakers, maybe that's how they kept up with him. They look forty or maybe even older.

"Another warm one?" the fat one asks, wincing an apology as he asks it.

"No thanks." Tyler has barely touched his first. It's in an unmarked green plastic bottle and, though he's never had homemade beer before, he can taste that that's what it is.

"The tea's pretty close." The fat one lifts the kettle from the woodstove, as if in doing this he can assess how close it is to boiling. Well, maybe he can, Tyler sees, maybe he can feel water-roil through the handle.

"Man, we really need another screen," the ponytail one complains. Only one window has a screen, and with the wood-stove on he'd wanted to open the door for a cross-draft, but at night apparently the bugs are awful.

Out the windows, it's completely dark. Tyler pictures his mother and Kim with insects awful around them. His mother refuses to use repellant. They will have a fire going by now. *Natural light.* Tyler is all they are talking about. They are a mix of afraid and angry and repentant. They know he has no flash-light and beyond their little fire all is dark. His mother, of course, is mostly afraid. How will little Tyler get back from his *little walk.* He remembers her face as she said this, as she said it not looking at Tyler but at Kim, her face pink with beer and naughty, shitty fun.

He's been here in the cabin for at least an hour now. His ribs feel better. The fat one's salve is amazingly soothing. His "famous elf balm" he called it, and Tyler didn't want to let him try it on him but he was still afraid of them then. The fat one said it was made of wild beeswax and sap from Douglas fir and chocolate lily, something his sister made and sold.

"Sorry," Tyler asks now. "What are your names again?"

"Bab," says the ponytail one, pointing to his chest. "And that's Lawrence."

"It's . . . *Bab*?" Tyler asks.

"One of those jokes that sticks," Bab explains.

"You sure you don't want a ride back?" Lawrence asks, lifting the tea kettle again.

"Not yet. A while maybe."

"You don't think they're worried?"

Tyler shrugs and says nothing.

"How's the leg now?"

"It's okay." Tyler lifts his right leg for them and twirls the sandaled foot, which hurts to do, maybe enough to make him limp. He doesn't remember hurting it. Maybe when he jumped the creek. Maybe when the deer fence got him.

At the marijuana field, after they'd helped him to his feet, their main concerns were, one, that he might come back and steal their plants, or, two, that he'd tell the Vietnamese and they would "Hang our balls from trees," Bab had joked. Tyler was convincing in his apologies and also in his assurances that he didn't smoke pot, or know anyone who even knew anyone who was Vietnamese. He was only here camping with his mother. This fact seemed to sum him up for them because both Bab and

Lawrence quietly exhaled, Ahhh, at ease now. Tyler went on to say that he'd gone walking, got sort of lost, found their place, and was looking for a phone to call his mother's cell. Both men said Ahhh again, and they didn't seem angry any more.

Getting to their cabin, putting a warm beer in his hand, Lawrence had gone for the elf balm and a wash cloth while Bab came up with an idea to keep Tyler quiet about their farm. He had tried, for a minute, to act tough.

"Okay," he said as Lawrence appeared with damp cloth and the flat tin of salve, "I want to see some I.D."

"My I.D.?"

"Let's see some."

Tyler took his wallet out and Bab told Lawrence to get him a pen. Bab found Tyler's social insurance card and library card and Lawrence handed Bab a pen. Bab sent Lawrence back for some paper.

"Okay, *Tyler*," Bab said, reading the name, serious. "We know who you are and where you live." In the background, Lawrence snorted at this. He opened the flat tin of balm, smelled it, poked a gentle finger in, and then rubbed some on his sunburned nose.

"So if we see any plants missing, we know who. And we know where. Okay?"

"Okay."

"And if, and if the cops come, we'll know . . ." Bab looked around, stumped, a smile breaking out.

"We'll know who to yell at from prison," Lawrence offered.

"That's *right*," Bab told Tyler, smiling, stab-pointing at his face.

"I'm really not going to tell anybody," Tyler said.

"Look," said Bab, folding the piece of paper and putting it in his shirt pocket, "we're being *nice* to you, right?"

THE NIGHT WINDOW   21

"Right."

"I mean we're just all good humans here so just don't tell anyone, 'cause we'll get hurt, okay?"

"I really won't."

"Good. Thanks." Bab looked at him closely. "How old are you anyway? Fourteen?"

"Sixteen."

"You want a ride back to the lake?"

"No, not yet. I can't. Quite yet." Tyler hesitated then told them why, and they laughed, but not unsympathetically. Lawrence gave him a little squeeze on the shoulder, and then Frisbeed the tin of balm onto his lap as he walked past.

When Tyler asked if they lived here all the time, he was told it was their "summer residence," and that they farm — their word — here in the summer and tour in the winter. Lawrence then explained that "toured" sounded grandiose, that actually it was more travelling than touring, meaning playing music and getting paid for it. They always went to warm places. They'd recorded an early independent album and in the last decade two CDs but, no, there's no way Tyler would have heard of them. But Bab passed him a CD case and there they were on the cover. They were "Jones." No, they weren't brothers. It was a name, said Bab, "that seemed cool eighty years ago." All this led to Tyler saying he'd love to hear their music, but with the generator down a CD was impossible, which led to them rooting around in back for what instruments they had there and, after apologizing that this wasn't their good gear, they began to play. First they gave him a CD to keep, he has it here under his hand and he keeps picking it up and studying it. Bab and Lawrence are younger on the cover, but it's them.

Tyler figures he's been gone a few hours now. Bab and Lawrence are into their second song when Tyler decides that these two are the kindest men he has ever met. They seem genuinely to like that he's here. Bab plays guitar and Lawrence a mandolin, the sound of which Tyler describes to himself as rows of tiny angel bells. First they played "Turn, Turn, Turn," harmonizing beautifully, softer and gentler than in the old Byrds' song, and Bab's guitar — he explains — is tuned to sound like a twelve-string. This second song is their own composition and it also forefronts their harmonies, which they love to perform and which are truly sweet. One of the lines in the sad chorus is, "Just another waya prayin."

Tyler finishes the gigantic bowl of tortilla chips in front of him. A hand-carved, clover-shaped bowl holds three kinds of dip. The bean dip is the best he's ever had. Lawrence insisted on heating it up a little first, saying it's three times as good warm, something about "luring out the earth in it." Tyler also has a glass of homemade blackberry wine in front of him. It sounded good but it isn't and he's had only a sip. It sits beside the full beer. Lawrence and Bab have been puffing marijuana from a small pipe, Bab offering it once with raised eyebrows but not asking again. It doesn't seem to affect them other than they've stopped talking much at all and sometimes they chuckle at jokes Tyler doesn't catch. They seem to talk with their music. Once during the last song they were staring at each other quizzically, then Bab dipped his head and did a little something with a bass string, and Lawrence laughed and said, "*That?*"and this was the only word in the conversation.

His mother, he knows, would love them. She would. There is no doubt in Tyler's mind that she would love these two guys. His mother would love everything in this cabin.

They are into their fifth or sixth song when Tyler sees what he's been waiting all evening to see. Kim's muscular high-beams violate the whole forest with false daylight then turn into the drive and momentarily hurt his eyes.

She's been a long time coming. He wonders how many wrong logging roads were taken, if they fought much, and how difficult she found the sporadic track of beer cans he'd left for her beside the road. He understands that his father didn't leave any cans.

The SUV stops behind the pickup midway up the drive, a door opens and but doesn't close and the beam of Tyler's reading light bounces toward him — his mother must be running.

Tyler bets the candles must look pretty eerie from out there. The reading light runs nearer then slows and stops at the biggest window and there is his mother's face, dim, pressed to the glass. She's alone and frantic and — compared to the good things going on here in this cabin — of another world.

GARGOYLES

I t's two or three but he isn't asleep. Propped on an elbow he peers out his window at the noise. Down on the street, under the street light whose braying he detests, a panel van has inched up to the curb. Under such light it's hard to tell if the van is silver, or white, or even yellow. He decides to see it as white. He can tell from a sudden lack of something that the van has been turned off. Three men get out. The third one, the driver, trots to catch up to the others, his stomach jiggling in a T-shirt that's either white or yellow. The driver carries a hammer.

He lights a candle and turns to his bedside table, the old radio and its parts spread out over the butcher paper. It's an odd thing to have in a bedroom, but all his work now takes place here. Such a scatter so close to his head while he sleeps — he wonders if it affects his dreams. The radio is from the 1930s or 1940s, and unlike the circuit boards of today has lots of parts. Some of the screws are so small, some of the washers so paper-thin that he sees himself in a fit of hearty snoring maybe breathing something in. It's a beautiful old radio, high deco, its shoulders — what would be its shoulders if a radio had shoulders — made of an early plastic, naively but confidently grooved, its colour an attempt at ivory. The radio's shell and its dissembled parts flicker in the candlelight. It looks rather Frankenstein-like. He doesn't know what else to do with this radio, how much more he can take it down. He doubts he can get the tubes apart without breaking the glass.

He wonders what the men outside will think of the radio. Or the project glued onto his bedroom wall — the pocket watch, one of his early dissemblies. Every piece, almost sixty, some so small he can't see them in this light, stuck to the wall in a pattern that was his best effort at patternlessness. Now he sees fractals. To the two friends who had occasion to see this paste-up he offered the word "installation." The friends just nodded, and he suffered a dip of dismay that they didn't know he was joking. As if at seventy-seven he had the arrogance to change careers and say he's now a visual artist. As if he'd call a childish paste-up "art." It's tragic you can get this old and people you call friends don't know when you're joking. He wonders what the three men below will see when his dissembled watch falls under their flashlight beams — a starscape? golden snow? — or if it will register in their eyes at all.

He checks for them out the window. They are behind the rhododendrons, looking up. He doubts they can see him. They look afraid. As they should.

The dissembling itself was no joke. Taking the watch apart was only serious. He'd chosen such a small object as a challenge to age, had gone out and purchased jeweller's tools and an eyeglass. He remembers tweezing that first piece, trying not to shake, pulling it gently away from its neighbour piece and away from the whole. Making it bigger by making space. It's a new architecture, a purest architecture he's learning, one that widens the spirit. In the stomach a palpable emptiness and glow. Each piece taken from a whole is another door lifted off hinges.

He falls back onto his pillow. He's breathing hard for no reason except age. He wonders if he shouldn't put on some clothes for this.

Richard interrupts the silence to give the taxi driver a second address. He really should see the house. How long has it been since he came out for Christmas? Three years? Four?

His accent heavy, the driver is squat and feline and could come from any number of hot countries. He appears irritated by the detour, as if he's being asked something that threatens his wallet, though the meter ticks steadily up. When Richard spots the house and asks the driver to slow down, the driver swings to him with apparent dismay and asks, "You *want*?"

It doesn't help that the house the driver has been asked to stop at is doorless, with dark gaps like empty eye sockets. Through the front door, furniture can be seen in the hall shadows. Even the double garage door is gone. The perimeter of the house is barred with two strips of yellow police tape and Richard doesn't bother to explain when the driver turns again to stare at him. He takes in this house he hardly knows, the helpless little curve of its drive, meant to suggest an estate. The faux shutters. He wonders why, ten or twelve years ago, his parents ended up here, in suburbs. They had lived in Barcelona. New York. New Mexico. Up a fjord ten miles from the Alaskan border. Likely they were here for the same reason as everybody else — convenience. Proximity to a hospital.

Richard wonders if the police were calling the home invasion a home *invitation* because of the absence of doors. Well, why wouldn't they joke? Isn't his father's eccentricity funny? Or, if we just cut to it and call it dementia, what's dementia except nature's ugliest joke? To put the wrinkling people back in diapers and also make them crazy.

He wonders if he has the legal right to go in and look around. Though why bother. He's been in a thousand houses like it, sold dozens with a similar floor plan.

Richard remembers the trips, which were always in service to his father's career, where he first learned about the qualities of the desirable home. All those times as a child hanging around odd buildings, learning concepts like "natural light" and "onsite-energy source." He remembers that long drive to New Mexico when, leaving a gas station, him in the back seat with a new old-fashioned pop bottle in hand, his father explained "neo" to him. And when he arrived at their new home he understood that "Neo Vernacular" meant a huge old weathered country shack that was actually brand new and had heated floors, disguised solar panels, and a cool hidden electric dumbwaiter that delivered stuff up to his bedroom.

This house, his father's last, had no architectural label.

Richard wonders at the house's worth, and the size of his commission. Because of course he'll be getting the listing. Why wouldn't he? He isn't up on the market here but it's in a nice neighbourhood and might be in the half-million range.

But how perverse is this? To hear about his father's attack, to fly out and pass the house on his way to his distraught mother — and then to pause and calculate commission? He feels some guilt, but wishes he felt more.

When told to continue downtown, the driver groans as if put upon.

He can't find his robe in the dark of the closet so he feels for candles in his drawer and locates two. They are the Gaudi tower replicas a colleague sent from Barcelona as a kitschy joke; from the look of it Gaudi wanted to build a vertical city for hobbits. Space hobbits. Catholic space hobbits.

He now must go back to his bedside table for the matches. He's still getting used to the non-electric life. Nearing the window, absurdly, he covers his bare groin with cupped hands, though everything he covers is grey as a ghost. In any case, the men are no longer where they were.

He goes to the closet again and, forgetting, flips the dead light switch. Then, cursing, returns to the bedside table, grabs the matches he's forgotten, and finally lights the candles. How is it possible to keep forgetting the same thing?

He does remember the breast that made him quit electricity. Not being a football fan he hadn't actually seen it, not live, but in the after-hubbub he saw replay after replay. He found it interesting that Canadian replays showed the breast, while American replays masked it with blur, like the face of an alleged felon. Actually it was the Canadian version he hated most. To see a breast treated like that. First, that it was encased in ugly armour, then revealed with sham violence. With that gesture, society got a sick self-portrait. And in their outrage that children had glimpsed a breast, the howling Bible-thumpers were just as sick. How has a breast become a dirty thing? How is it *possible*? Eleanor's breasts, he remembers encountering them that first time and feeling them in his soul as the heart of their difference — and to think that beauty itself could make him breathe quickly! Then the same breasts feeding Richard, this odd connection between mother and son, the taut nipple a kind of weaning umbilicus, granting a child its independence slowly. That a breast was sheathed in crust then ripped free and exposed as everyman's soft-brown-shit-of-desire, well, it made him want to quit humanity. He pictures himself up a forested slope roping together a functional hut, no power pole in sight, leading his young Eleanor through the door, under the hanging blanket, both of them barefoot on the cool swept clay. Eleanor's breasts will have at times seen the sun, but only when it was her whim, nothing to do with the mass neurosis-of-the-day. The TV breast wasn't even all that well shaped. It looked like a listless football. It occurs to him that maybe that's all he's complaining about here. He hopes he didn't go to the basement and kill the main switch and quit electricity because some celebrity's breast wasn't what he wanted it to be.

But that's that, no more electricity. He will learn what this life is like, and try to feel it as another opening. Hard, at first. For instance, he thinks he remembers his decision at night, and, after descending to the basement and locating the panel, the second he pulled the switch he found himself in the reality of a pitch-black cellar, against the cement wall most distant from the stairs, with no flashlight. But a promise was a promise and the switch stayed down, though he tripped once finding the stairs. The next day he got a taxi to deliver, along with a few groceries, a gross of candles. Then he had to phone a friend to bring over some matches.

The entrance to his mother's building sports an ostentatious royal blue awning that lacks only a smarmy doorman. Otherwise the building looks solid. How fancy does waterfront have to be? Richard finds her name on the panel and buzzes. Answering, her stilted voice betrays someone new to the system. She tells Richard her suite number is 631, then instructs him that it's on the sixth floor. Richard is reminded that his mother is eighty, then remembers she is capable of that kind of humour.

She greets him at the door and they hug. It's been at least three years, and again Richard is shocked by a body impossibly dwindled, a bony baby bird, with a fledgling's baldness too. Her eyes have gained an odd creaminess and colour, the slight blue of milk. He's been suffering this shock-of-age since she was fifty, ever since he'd stopped living in their city, but how can it surprise him so deeply every time?

His mother makes her way back across the living room to sit in a chair angled toward the picture window. Richard steps up beside her, takes in the million-dollar view of the harbour. In the near distance a sea plane takes off, though one can hear nothing. Sailboats creep along under power, some coming in from the wind, others going out to find it. He sees waterfront signs for a wax museum, an undersea world, some hotels.

"I've always wanted this," his mother says.

"I can see why," Richard responds neatly, pretending not to hear the weight in her voice.

Adding even more weight, she lifts a beer bottle off the windowsill and sips from it. His mother, who never drank. Never, in all the years with his father, who enjoyed it almost to the point of abuse, who tried to get her to join him. Richard finds this beer of hers spectacularly perverse but he says nothing.

"And how's Melanie?" his mother asks.

"She's fine. She's good." How *is* Melanie? She's fine.

"Give her my love when you phone her to report on things."

"I will." The nose of a huge ship has come into view. White, a cruise ship. "How long have you been here again?"

"Right after the doors came off."

"And how long has —"

"I put up with the blankets for about a week."

"Right."

"I couldn't sleep. The first week a storm came right in our front hall, blew over the coat rack, and stained the antique hutch."

"I know. We talked on the phone, Mom. About those blankets."

She meets his eye in a way that says, If that is so, why didn't you fly out and make things right? He wants to tell her that, at the time, he didn't — he really didn't — think it was that serious. During another, ritual phone call, his father had laughed explaining the blankets. His mother was in the background and she wasn't screaming or crying. Richard knew she was scared, but he chalked that up to being less adventurous with age. He knew his father was being conceptual again, but he didn't know how dangerously conceptual.

"I checked in here three months ago this week."

"This is a condo, right, Mom?"

"Yes. And the furniture was all here. And dishes for eight. Though I haven't entertained. Well, just Dorothy that one time. New Year's Eve we shared a bottle of wine she brought over. The cork almost took her head off!"

"You didn't spend New Year's Eve with Dad?"

"He didn't spend New Year's Eve with me." His mother turns almost completely away to continue her watch over the small harbour.

Richard reaches down to take her elbow and squeeze it. She doesn't respond.

"So, Mom, did you buy this place? Or are you renting?"

"I'm —" She stiffens, momentarily confused. A little spasm seems to help and, finding the word, she turns to him, angry with him for asking.

"It's a lease."

Richard nods, not knowing what to say, except, "It's nice."

"It has a door."

"Right."

"When your father had our doors removed? And they were just awful empty holes? He called them his gargoyles."

"Gargoyles?"

"That was it for me."

Richard easily recalls the summer at the lake when his father taught him about gargoyles. Gargoyles became a large part of that summer and several beyond. He remembers coming upon his father late one night, sketching under the coal-oil lamp. Even then his father embraced the old-fashioned. There at the lake, neighbours found his oil lamps more quaint than strange.

His father was chuckling while sketching. Richard braved an interruption — he was in his pyjamas, he was supposed to be in bed — to see what was so funny. In lamplight his father's round, tanned face shone deep orange, and his cheeks and chin where he hadn't shaved fell almost to black and made him a little frightening. He was sketching with two of Richard's pencil crayons, a brown and a grey. What looked to be a series of hunched dragons was, his father explained, a creature called a gargoyle.

"I like that one with his eyes closed," Richard said, pointing, not quite touching the paper. You weren't to touch Dad's drawing, though these didn't look like his work-drawing.

"He's supposed to be squinting."

"I like that fat one too. How his tongue curls like that."

"Do you think it's too long for a tongue?"

"Make it even longer," Richard said, only happy to be asked. "But how come they're all sitting like that?"

"They're squatting. On the ledge of a building. In this case a cottage. I'm designing a summer cottage, next lake over, and the client wants," his father snorted and shook his head, "four gargoyles. One for each corner eave. Actually you'd call this cottage a country estate. But I don't think the project will happen."

His father explained that no two gargoyles were alike. They were creatures of the imagination. If you travelled Europe you could see them on the oldest buildings. Yes, they often had their tongues out, or their claws, and in some cultures, their penises. They were trying to look ugly on purpose, because they were actually protectors, protectors of your home. Their job was to scare away evil spirits.

"What did the evil spirits look like?"

"You mean what *do* they look like?" And here his father put his round, orange face close to Richard's and looked scary-on-purpose, like a devil.

That summer Richard began making gargoyles himself. What began as a joke around the dinner table became a real project for him, and a dizzying leap for his artwork, which up till now had graced merely the refrigerator. His father was not only letting him carve gargoyles for the eaves of their cottage, but encouraging him to. His mother protested that gargoyles would ruin the look of a cottage. To her more subtle hints that a ten-year-old might not be capable of turning out art worthy of adorning "not just a playhouse, but a place someone lives," his father said, "What do we care?" This gave even young Richard pause, for wasn't caring about that exactly what an architect did?

His father bought carving tools and showed how every single cut had to be away from your body. He chainsawed the roughest of shapes for him, based on Richard's preliminary sketch. Cedar was one of the easiest woods to carve, he explained, and had natural preservative in its sap, which was why it lasted so long, years and years, even unpainted, and which was why it was used for totem poles, and why it would be perfect for his gargoyle. This was Richard's proudest moment of the summer, hearing that his father wanted his gargoyle to last. His first, which did indeed end up on a corner eave of their cottage, had a single bent horn on his forehead. He was fat, and smiling. His impossible tongue was too big and fat to be a tongue at all and looked like a second head. Gouged eyebrows formed a V above his nose to show any evil spirits how mean he would be if they got close.

Even now, decades later, Richard can see every homely, botched detail of his first gargoyle. Whenever he smells cedar, he sees that face emerging, smiling and mean, from the tortured wood. What was frustrating, but then not, was how different it was from what he'd drawn. At first he hated that he couldn't carve very well. Then he learned to see that the gargoyle had always had its own idea of its face and it wasn't going to behave. Because that's what gargoyles were like. They might sit up on your house for you, but there's no way they would ever behave.

He hears faint footsteps and, he thinks, whispering. His thumb is bleeding pretty badly. He had momentarily sat himself down at his radio dissembly, inspired to pry the metal collar from a glass tube, and the glass gave way in his grip, imploding with a *chuck*, cutting his thumb. He has been sitting watching his blood, its beading up to form a drip, which grows heavy enough for gravity to take across his wrist, leaving a black trail, and *plick*, onto the tabletop. Five drips so far. It is slowing, clotting. He smiles at the final bead. Will it or won't it? Such a tentative dissembling. He wouldn't have the patience for it.

So, the men are inside. They're in the house, he's in danger, and Eleanor was right. She is always right. The outside did come in. His guess had been that no one would dare.

He hears them down there whispering. Which means they are afraid. So he's still right. He's still right.

As is Eleanor. As are the men downstairs. Everyone's right. Everyone's always right. Isn't that funny? He does believe exactly this impossibility: one may be deluded or mistaken but at one's inmost core everyone's always right. He thinks he truly understands this to be the human condition. He also understands his version to be far more tragic than the other one, that of original sin, which is nothing more than the church's cheap bait. The tragedy is that, though we are all completely right, it's hard to know what to *do*.

So the men are inside. So, his gargoyles have failed. But probably they were made impotent only because their secret was made known. His mistake had been to hire out labour, a carpenter with no allegiance to the project, and who no doubt had gone right off to the nearest pub to bellow details of this oddest of jobs, that he'd been well paid to haul away every door in the house, plus plaster over all recessions and screw holes, and replace these doors with nothing. And of course it would filter out that there was nobody inside this newly doorless house but a rickety old coot alone upstairs. Plus the carpenter had that little helper come out for the garage door, that's right, and it's not hard to imagine them in any number of bars, laughing about it. And so goes the secret behind the doorless house. Mystery is a gargoyle's only power.

You'd think the mystery of no doors would be limitless.

He should have done the damn doors himself. His mistake was to doubt that he was up to lifting doors and mixing spackle. No, his *real* mistake had been age.

He stands, almost falling. Stiff at the radio for too long, his shoulder has seized and he is crooked with no balance. He loosens up by the time he reaches the closet, where he chooses the gold silk robe instead of the white terrycloth. The silk robe lacks a waist tie, and he is wearing no underwear — he is glad and a little proud to see he still has a sense of humour despite three men crossing his threshold and invading his house.

He hears hoarse whispers — *laptop* and *cut the fuckin' cable*. They are taking the expected things. In their mousey rustling he can hear that his gargoyles worked in part. They aren't barging about fearlessly. Drawers are being slid out with care. Cupboard doors are silent on their hinges.

It doesn't sound like they will be coming upstairs at all. So he will go down to them. He will confront the men with openness, welcome them into the logic of expansion, wherein no evil can survive. The men will either run or become odd friends.

Richard watches his mother tilt her head back to empty the beer, the universal gesture so unlike her. She rises and takes the bottle to the kitchen, depositing it under the sink in a manner that tells him she won't have another today but will tomorrow.

At her new fridge she rests her fingertips on its surface as if to reacquaint herself.

"Are you hungry? Would you like something to eat?"

"No thanks. I ate on the flight."

"You *did*?" Mock horror, an old family joke. He actually likes airplane food.

It's amazing she can find humour at all, given what has

happened. But maybe not so amazing, maybe it says that all her years with him have been an emergency and that yesterday's debacle was simply the emergency continuing. In fact maybe what he was witnessing here wasn't the collapse of a monumental relationship but rather a last shard hitting the ground, and the settling dust.

Richard can only imagine the two of them in recent years. His father growing quietly wilder, his mother concerned with security to the point of paranoia. He does see this all the time with older purchasers and perhaps it makes sense: the less life to lose, the more one wants to protect it. His mother has always been afraid of encroaching crime, the inner city crawling out. He remembers her locking car doors, even taxi doors, when she drove through a downtown, particularly its grubby perimeter. He recalls his father, in a family discussion about a next new place to live, asking if she would like him to design her "a castle with a clear view of the peasantry coming up the slope."

Gazing out the window he eventually registers the school of kayakers he's been staring at. They look tentative. He thinks he can make out grey heads. His mother is slowly spooning and tinking something into a teapot. What was it like for her when the doors first came off and the blankets hung? Listening to his father during that call, Richard actually thought it a cool idea, at least a funny idea.

"Okay, Richard, picture this," was how his father put it, his voice pocked with the years but his confidence as robust as ever. "You're a thief, a bad guy. You're walking down a street, a suburban street. You're casing it. You pass a house with *no doors*. Instead it has *blankets* hung over the door holes. You're a thief. Is that the place you pick to rob? Would you rob that place?" The question's rhetorical, but his father waits. All his life, Richard has had to answer the rhetorical questions too.

"I dunno."

"No. You wouldn't. Why? Because a person who uses only a blanket has no worries about safety. You're a thief and you see this house and you imagine this unbelievable monster living in there behind those blankets. Right?"

"I guess."

"Maybe it's a guy just waiting for someone to *try*. You wouldn't go in there if you were paid to. Someone who feels safe living behind a blanket is a witch or a maniac. No way you're wandering in there to steal their stuff."

He had a carpenter lift the doors off, up went the blankets, and his mother had stayed for a while. It must have been a final torture for her. Apparently the blankets were authentic Navajo, flown in on this whim of his, and expensive. And then a month or so later — his mother isn't clear on this, though his father had phoned her at her new condo to explain — he'd had the carpenter come back to remove the blankets, and the garage door too, even plastering over all the holes from screws and hinges and locks. Smooth, pristine entranceways.

Richard knows her torture was only a side issue, a by-product. Of his art. His art was all. It always had been. In fact it was maybe her paranoia that triggered this particular project in the first place. Him trying to prove something to her. It was perverse and juvenile and it failed. Richard remembers another prank that was also probably a reaction to his mother, in that house — they called it a hacienda — his father reno'd while they lived in it, on the north California coast. He built a family room extension to include a living redwood tree that was four feet in diameter. To accommodate movement, not so much from growth but from wind, he found some kind of space-age gasket for the roof-hole, a kind of putty that adjusted itself. Grandson of Flubber, his father called it. Richard grew to love that tree, its cavernously grooved bark. It had as strong a presence as a person. But he suspected even then — and he's more suspicious now — that the idea arose out of his mother's loud fear of ticks in the area and the serious fever they gave you. Is it possible the tree was his father's perverse response? That his bringing the threat inside was just another sign of his parents' nauseating marital warp?

"It's reebus," says his mother, and Richard has no idea what she means by this. Perhaps it's the tea she's making.

Richard tries to make what he says next sound as little like criticism as possible and it comes out almost chatty. "So you haven't seen him yet?"

His mother turns from the kitchen counter. Kettle steam tumbles up beside her face. She takes Richard in, not answering, but her expression is plain. Why would she visit him, no matter what shape he was in? Why visit a man who, after fifty years of marriage, would treat her this way? Despite her pleas, despite her promise that she would leave if he actually did remove the doors — he just went ahead and removed them. Should she visit such a man?

"I haven't."

"Do you think you might want to?"

Again no answer. He is afraid to tell her that in ten minutes he is going to leave, and visit him. He hasn't foreseen this, that she might feel as deserving of his time as his father, though he lies wounded and deranged in a hospital.

"Mom. Obviously he hasn't been himself. What he did was cruel, I know, but he isn't cruel. He hasn't been himself."

"Well, maybe it's time I wasn't myself too."

He thinks for a moment that she is going to stick her tongue out.

"Mom, I'm not going to try to talk you into it. But they say he might have had some sort of stroke. He has a head injury. And a hand injury."

"They've kept me informed."

"Well. Okay."

"He can visit me when he's better."

"Well, no, I think he's sick, Mom. Before this." He doesn't want to say what he thinks, because to insult him is still to insult her.

"He doesn't have dementia, Richard."

"You don't think?"

"He was cruel to you too. He was. You know he was. And now, now he's been very cruel to me."

Richard rises and passes her in her small kitchen, her "galley" it's probably called in this oceanfront building. He can come to her kitchen and root around in a cupboard because she's his mother and that's what sons can always do. He puts his hand on a can of bing cherries. He knows she means his father mocking him, early on, for choosing to sell real estate. For selling instead of creating. Choosing, as his father put it, "to drive people around, wipe their bums, take their money." But he never thought his father was shaming him so much as he was trying to get him to change his mind. There's a huge difference. In any case, if shame is what it was, it didn't stick. And it's hard to say that to a mother, that a son could live a few thousand miles away and no longer think of his parents much, even if he's been shamed. Perhaps especially if he's been shamed.

It hasn't occurred to him in years, but when he first started selling, he did feel shame because of his father, though a different sort. It had to do with what he had learned from him. When he took clients into a backyard, shrugged at a tangle of wild shrubs and described a tight bank of cedar in its place, or pointed out a bay window or deck where there wasn't one, and he saw the buyers' eyes fix and understand, he was seeing the world as his father saw it and using his father's words. He was also proving again one of capitalism's open secrets, that fortunes are made from others' lack of imagination. That he was straight and male seemed to add credibility: if *he* could see aesthetic improvements they must be essential. It happened again and again. How many times had he made a sale and gained the seller fifty thousand by insisting they first spend ten thousand to add a dropped half-deck and hot tub? Timid purchasers would step through the sliders and see not a shitty backyard neighbourhood but instead a dropped deck and tub, and a little breathlessly see themselves as wine-clinking success stories, naked and beautiful in their tub, and they could see friends and bosses seeing them too. It was all about painting a picture for those who couldn't paint their own. Sometimes he left his black convertible in the client's driveway, nose pointed out, and sometimes he didn't. Sometimes he insisted that certain curtains be closed. He installed tastefully unique screen savers on his clients' computers. Essential oils — tangerine was best — he dabbed under homely kitchen counters like perfume near an armpit. He always suggested there be no children around, and that all but one good toy be hidden. It was what his father called "the built environment." In Richard's business, colleagues saw it both as manipulation and as service, and no one — not even purchasers these days — saw any contradiction.

"Richard?"

He is standing over her in her chair. His hand rests on her shoulder and she has put a hand over his to keep it there.

"What."

"He doesn't have dementia, Richard. He's working."

At the top of the stairs he's aware of the shifting facets of himself. He's aware of vestigial anger, a lingering bile that wants him to stomp down there and yell *get the fuck out of my house you low-life bastards*. Several deeply quiet breaths take care of it for now. Another part of him wants to be entertained, wants to come upon them as if casually, tell them to please do help yourselves, yes, take those electronics specifically, I no longer have a use for them, too much nudity on TV these days, so yes, please, do me the favour of carting everything away. Another part of him wants to appear from out of the shadows, gnarly, old, and clearly unafraid. And then of course a wheedling part, a part he has to breathe through as well, wants to run back to his room, lie down, cover up, hide, wait.

But he takes a first step down. As he does so he almost falls, for in his stepping he has understood, for the first time, the genius of a staircase. Squares of wood fit perfect against squares of space — harlequin squares. Sized to fit the human stride, they ascend and descend, impossibly, at the same time. Up and down both, always and eternally, and very alive at their fulcrum of stillness.

The cab driver has buzzed, Richard and his mother have hugged. His hand is on her doorknob but he stops because she is going to say something more. Behind her head, the cruise ship is being pushed sideways into a pier by three tugs.

"He thinks I'm afraid but he's the one who's afraid." She

stares through Richard's chest, angry. She brings her hands up and clenches both into fists. "He's afraid, Richard. Do you know that? He's afraid of his feelings. Do you *know* —" She pauses, looks up at him, appears to be registering his face at the cost of forgetting her words. She has to look away to find her train of thought. "— Do you know he could not watch the movies? Never could? Never tried again?"

She keeps her gaze on his chest and appears satisfied and finished, so Richard must say, "What do you mean?"

"The family movies he took. Remember? With the old camera? The home movies."

His father had always had the best possible video camera — early on, a Super-8 — for walking around a structure so he could see how it "moved," as the light, shadow, and background changed as he circled it. Once in a while he pointed it at Richard and his mother. Richard has seen them all once or twice, though not in twenty, thirty years. He remembers favourite shots, his father water-skiing and falling cartoonishly for the camera. A sequence of Richard at the same cottage, ten or eleven, a chisel-wound from carving, a palm gouged and proudly displayed for the camera, the young machismo. Holding his hand up and waving, a blood bead coursing down his wrist. On film it looked black.

"He's never, never, been able to watch you. I saw him try once, and he looked miserable and he cried. I don't know if he sees your life flying by or his life flying by, but he can't stand it." Eleanor is teary now too. "Can't see you as a little boy. Simply can't stand it."

Richard is unable to tell whether his mother is crying out of sympathy for her husband or out of the same horror, seeing time die.

He starts down the sacred stairs, treading softly with new respect. He hasn't heard the men for a minute but he senses they haven't left. He doesn't know why he feels so weak but he does, and it's all he can to do to keep gravity from helping him too quickly to the bottom of the stairs.

He no longer knows what he might do or say and even less what he *should* do or say. All plans are off, mostly because a plan will change in any case — warp, distort, join the long dissembly that is the ongoing scatter and fade of his mind. Thoughts, they rise, have their say and then fade, all thoughts are the same in this, none are more than others, even the ones that change the faces of buildings. Each thought, like this one, fading now. Into the image of a knee lifting and planting, descending a perfect set of stairs, which was once seen to be a miraculous machine. Some people were probably afraid of early stairs, like his mother had been of the telephone. Richard at three was newly afraid up on his shoulders, though as a baby he had loved it, he grabbed him hard by the hair, a pain you can hardly stand but love anyway. Yes, once he clomped down some stairs with Richie on his shoulders, the little guy squealing, almost ripping out his hair. Eleanor unable to look, afraid they would fall, speaking so sternly with her face averted, that panicked monotone of hers, she wouldn't dare a rambunctious syllable for fear it will make him trip and tumble, Richie fast in his hair like a monkey.

Someone stubs a toe in the dark, swears, hisses, *Gimme your light.*

And so, halfway down the stairs, he says to them through a smile, "Sorry." It *is* his fault they're labouring in darkness.

An intake of breath, a *Jesus.* A flashlight beam swings up, into his eyes, light's body strikes him and he begins to fall.

Taken in gravity's certain hand he lets care itself dissemble. And, time — another flashlight beam finds him, falling. As his hands come away, as his robe comes apart and widens, he sees what he must look like as he flies down to them.

At the front of the hospital is a wide fountain and Richard climbs the steps beside it. The air feels cooler for the planes of water running over slabs of smooth concrete. It's a '60s style his father dismissed, calling it "cubism for the masses." The moving mirrors of water make no noise at all, and Richard knows someone was proud to get it exactly so.

The ward he's directed to is not intensive care, as he had assumed, but geriatric.

When the elevator doors open he can smell an earthy something under the chemical germ-killer. He passes doors but won't look in. He hears soft moans from one room, whining babble from another, silence from most. He came with Melanie to a place like this to visit her mother, once.

Is his father here for good? All these old folks stuffed into sterile caverns, waiting for death. His father, so aware of his environment, claiming how environment *is* one's mood. He would find a hospital hellish for that alone.

At the nurse's station he gets pointed directions, is told a nurse is in with his father now. Richard finds the door and meets this nurse on her way out. He introduces himself to the short, young woman with a kind smile and tired but patient eyes. She is dressed mostly in what appears to be green disposable paper. She rustles when she moves.

"I had to dress his thumb again. It keeps bleeding because he won't stop wiggling it." She could be speaking about a child — isn't he naughty. "We might need to put in a stitch."

Richard needs her to back up into bigger things.

"He's had a stroke?"

"Well, now, the tests show nothing so far, but he's uncommunicative."

"Always was." Richard smiles to tell her it's a joke.

"He had a blow to the head. So we don't know if it's that, or it might be the shock, from the attack. He's, how old is he? Seventy-five?"

"Seventy-nine. He was definitely attacked? The doctor I spoke to says he may have fallen."

"Well, we don't know. The police report was very, was not very clear. A neighbour found him just as he was regaining —"

"My father won't say what happened?"

The nurse eyes him anew. Her manner softens.

"I think you have to see him yourself. He won't stop moving. He's hallucinating." The nurse has Richard by the arm, stopping him from going in quite yet. "I should warn you. There's lots of swelling."

His father is curtained off at the far end of the room. Sunlight enters such that Richard can see his father's shadow projected onto the curtain. He is sitting on the edge of his bed, and his hands are busy.

Richard doesn't pull the curtain aside but more quietly lifts and steps under. His father's face is badly swollen on one side and an eye socket is puffed and blackened. His nose might be broken. Other than that, it's his father, who has always looked old to him.

"Hi, Dad."

It's curious, his father's response to this. His hands keep working away in front of him. He turns his head to Richard's voice but his eyes stay down, keep staring at whatever it is his hands are working on. Turning in the sunlight, his face is cut hard with shadows.

"You feel okay?"

His father looks content enough. Nothing in his eyes suggests pain or suffering of any kind. He looks freshly cleaned, his hair combed. On his bedside table, an empty Dixie cup is torn into many pieces. A drinking straw with an accordion bend has been pulled straight and taut.

"Mom sends her love."

He realizes he does feel repelled. Not by his appearance so much. It's that his father still isn't talking to him, still isn't looking at him. His father who, sitting there, patiently working his hands, looks like a contented summary of himself.

Watching his father push whatever it is away, watching him nimbly combat the very air, Richard sees a perfect picture of futility. And he feels close to his father, as close as he ever has. He sees his father and knows himself: he lets no one in either.

Richard watches the hands. They are deft, and more articulate than his words ever were. They move, still, with delicacy and precision. Minutely pinching, pulling, sweeping. On second thought, he's not fighting the air. He's trying to clear it away. Not clear away — take apart.

THE KITE TRICK

This Tofino," pronounced Uncle Phil, from his bed, first cigarette of the day bouncing unlit in his lips, "is a freakish place."

It was warm and lovely out and the cause of his declaration, yesterday having been stormy and cold. "Hilariously cold," he had said, not laughing. "Mid-May?" He'd also found it freakish that you could always hear the roar of waves, the constant roar of waves.

"Cheers, mate."

Philip liked how his Uncle Phil thanked him. His uncle's namesake, he had fetched the cigarettes from the condo's living room, the kind of chore he'd been happily performing for two days, wanting to get to know his English uncle, his only uncle, whom he got to see once each year. Interesting, these notions of "relative" and "English." And Uncle Phil was entertaining in ways Philip's parents certainly weren't. Those expressions of his, for instance the way he sighed and said under his breath, "Deep carni*val*," pronouncing the second word like the French might. What did Uncle Phil mean by that?

From the doorsill Philip watched his uncle suck absently on his cigarette, take it out to discover its unlit end, then swear and lurch out of bed with more energy than he would show all day. Philip's mother wouldn't let Uncle Phil smoke inside the rented condo because of the children.

Uncle Phil still wore the bathing suit he'd worn last evening in the hot tub. He had the kind of body, Philip noted, that you expected of an English man, especially a musician, in that it was without defined muscle. Even his uncle's tan seemed not very attached to its skin, and mismatched to the pale tone underneath. Philip had to agree with his mother, whom he'd overheard telling his father that "Your brother is two years younger and looks ten years older." She'd said it accusingly, and Philip knew this had to do with his uncle's lifestyle. Or, as she put it, "How your brother lives."

"We did it backwards, darling," Uncle Phil shouted again to Aunt Sally, who didn't hear because she was out at the car "searching the boot" for sunscreen. By backwards he meant they shouldn't have gone to Jamaica before Canada, because "the other way 'round wouldn't have felt so freaking frigid. Next year we do cold *then* hot." Uncle Phil said "freaking" a lot and slipped occasionally. At each slip Philip's mother closed her eyes, and once took his father away for a hissing talk.

They sat eating breakfast quickly, Philip's little sister and brother racing to lick jam off their toast before they were told to stop. Philip's mother was impatient at the stove, waiting for the bacon to cook. Uncle Phil always wanted bacon, crispy bacon. Philip enjoyed the way his uncle defended his sins: earlier this morning, announcing that she was off to the resort store and what would people like for breakfast, his mother had startled at Uncle Phil's, "Any deeply sustaining pork product!" booming from behind his closed bedroom door. There was something so English in what he said, sly like the book *Winnie the Pooh* was sly.

The idea this morning was that Philip's mother and father and Aunt Sally would go whale-watching while Uncle Phil took the three kids to the main beach to enjoy the warm day. Twelve, Philip was old enough to appreciate the rather undramatic grey whales surfacing to breathe, but he got seasick even on calm water and in any case he had to help, as his father put it, "poor Uncle Phil look after the hordes." Uncle Phil did look grateful that Philip was staying behind. He and Aunt Sally had no children — another side of Uncle Phil that seemed to rub his mother wrong.

Eating bacon, pretending to try to entice them away from whale-watching, Uncle Phil said, "You're actually choosing the big grey blobs over 'the kite trick'?" He refused to tell anyone what the trick was, though Aunt Sally nodded while she confirmed, "It's a good one."

After breakfast, his parents and Aunt Sally gone, Philip stood in the bedroom door again to watch his uncle pull a canvas hunting vest over a bright red long-sleeved T-shirt and clutch himself, saying, "*Brrrr.*" He enjoyed being watched. His hair was always wild, standing up in strands that shifted comically as he moved. He would stay the whole day in that hunting vest — it had bullet holders and was apparently the real thing. On its back was a big yin-yang symbol, though two shades of blue rather than the typical black and white. Philip knew what it meant — it meant opposites that made a whole. Though odd on a hunting vest it was one of the more sensible ornaments.

He hated it when people said *ying*-yang. He hated people who used "phenomena" as the singular even more.

Philip backed out of the room when his uncle found a lighter in a vest pocket. But the smell of smoke followed him, almost instantly it seemed, as he walked past his sister and brother to open a window and the door to the patio. Though he performed these acts of ventilation quietly he felt awkward, a sissy in his mother's camp. Plus it was clear that these openings simply pulled the smoke more quickly out of Uncle Phil's bedroom and on into everyone's noses. No matter, Philip's mother would smell it, and tonight there would be more hissing out in the parking lot.

"So," said Uncle Phil, ambling out of the bedroom with cigarette blazing, unaware of his rebellion. "This famous 'Long Beach.' Will it have a mosh pit?"

"For sure." Ever since his uncle found out that Philip knew what a mosh pit was, and that his mother and father didn't, he talked this way. So does this famous "Grade 7" of yours have a mosh pit? So does this so-called "seafood restaurant" we're off to have a mosh pit? Philip and his uncle refused to reveal to the others what a mosh pit was. Aunt Sally, who had tattoos, would just sit quietly smiling. Philip could tell she didn't want to be here. Her eyes were steady with waiting. She was younger than Uncle Phil, and Philip knew they weren't really married, though they had been together for as long as he could remember. Uncle Phil sometimes called her "Aunt Silly," which made Sasha and Tommy laugh, especially when Aunt Silly pulled a face to match, but it also confused them, because their parents never made fun like that in front of children.

Leaving for the whale-watching, his mother had taken Philip aside, both his shoulders under her hands, steering him into the rhododendron grove bordering the parking lot.

"You are at a beach, with very, strong, undertow," she'd said. "*Adults* drown there. *Never* let Tommy and Sasha out of your sight. Do *not* let them go in over their ankles. Today it's *sand-castles*." She looked over her glasses toward the condo and raised her eyebrows. "*You* are the boss." She squeezed his shoulders and repeated, "*You*."

Philip resented his mother for standing in the way of him and Uncle Phil. It was becoming clear to him that you could have a special feeling for relatives, beyond seeing the play of genes. This year, Philip had come to understand that Uncle Phil visited each year not just to see his only brother but also, more and more, to see him too. The way he'd hugged him second at the airport, the way he said, "*Hell*o, Namesake."

Philip liked this about his uncle, this potential and blossoming uncle-ness. Though already familiar with the word, he had reviewed "avuncular" in his *OED*.

It was a twenty-minute drive to Long Beach and Uncle Phil did only one joke about driving on the wrong side of the road, veering over the double yellow line when there was no other car in sight, then a goofy "Oops!" and gently veering them back. Philip's brother and sister were thrilled, though only Sasha, eight, had any sense of there being a left or a right side to anything.

"I *can't* believe in one month you'll be *thirdeen*." Uncle Phil gave him a wink. "Thir*deen* is when it begins, mate."

Philip sat saying nothing. He smiled like his aunt smiled, tired and knowing. He knew what his uncle was on about. But he knew even better that, as far as "it" went, next year would be no different than this one.

"You have some fun but you keep up those famous straight A's of yours. All right? Get all yer girlfriends to help ya?"

"Sure."

"Promise?"

"Sure."

"You really got one hundred percent in maths?"

"I guess." Actually he'd got one hundred and five, this impossibility due to his teacher's inane dangling of bonus points.

"*And* science?"

"I guess."

"*And* wankology?"

Philip smiled and stared straight ahead. He really wanted to be praised for his reading, which was, of course, untestable.

"Cheers, mate."

"Cheers."

"Jesus, you know, you're a loner just like your dad." When Philip didn't respond, Uncle Phil added, "Which is not a bad thing, not a bad thing at all."

"What do you mean," Philip asked, "when you say, 'deep carnival'? What does that mean, exactly?"

"It means" — Uncle Phil stared into the road and tried hard for his nephew — "It means, the strange and colourful activity of human meat. That's what it means. 'Exactly.'" He looked over at Philip. "Get it?"

"I guess."

The parking lot was nearly empty of cars. Anyone on this beach that planed vastly off to the right was swallowed up in its sheer size. Philip could see what might be a beach umbrella a half-mile away. Someone in blue and yellow walked the haze and hard sand of low tide but you couldn't tell if they were one person or two. Other than that, a small dog poked about the huge bleached logs that storms had tossed, over the years, at foot of the forest.

"This is *brilliant*," said Uncle Phil, standing with hands on hips, taking it in, having almost to shout over the roar of surf. "There's no one *here*! *Look* at this! You don't get this where your father and I come from!" The breeze put his hair back, flat for once.

Sasha and Tommy sat anguished in the car. Tommy bounced. Uncle Phil finally understood their set faces.

"Yes! You can get out!" He raised his hands over his head, astounded that they would still be sitting there. "Out! Run off! It's a beach!"

"Stay close!" Philip shouted at their backs. "Sasha — keep Tommy with you. We'll catch up."

Uncle Phil opened the trunk and emptied it of towels, lunch pack, kite. He asked Philip if they should bring the shovel and Philip told him how good it was for sand castles, how it let you build something sizable. He liked using words like "sizable" around Uncle Phil for the way they made him comically startle (hair jerking) and say something like, "My namesake's a freaking intellectual."

At the edge of the parking lot Uncle Phil stopped in the breeze to take in the scope of what he was about to enter. He seemed almost nervous. Something in his uncle's hesitation made Philip proud that he lived in Canada: empty and powerful, and dangerous for that. Philip hadn't been to Long Beach for two years and he liked it well enough, though the water was useless being so cold, like it had melted only seconds before. It numbed you completely.

"Your father didn't tell me! This is brilliant!"

His father seemed critical of Uncle Phil too, though he smiled warmly when he spoke of his little brother. This was him yearning for England and his own boyhood — so Philip's mother explained it to Philip. His father had left England for Canada at eighteen, had gone to university to become a civil servant with Canada Post. Uncle Phil had stayed in London and, as his father put it, never grown up. Philip recalled his mother's face when, a few months ago, happening upon a reality show on TV, she studied a long-haired old guy stuttering his words. Then she declared with sarcastic revelation to Philip's father, "Your brother wishes he were *Ozzy Osbourne*."

Uncle Phil used to play in bands — he was a bass player, mostly a session musician. His main claims to fame were his "jams" with certain rock stars Philip had actually heard of. Plus he'd been hearing the stories since he was born. Uncle Phil had been on stage with Elton John, once, and with Phil Collins for a whole European tour, and once with Denny Laine of Wings, formerly of Moody Blues. He'd played on two tracks of Charlie Watts's solo album, though neither track made the final cut. He was on an entire Ian Drury live album and apparently you could see him on the cover. There were others his father could list, plus plenty more stories about musicians that weren't about music. Phil "knew the *first* guy who found Hendrix in the morning." He himself had "bodily saved a mature but severely pissed Richard Starkey from taking out an entire table loaded with pints."

It had been twenty years since Uncle Phil had played. Since then he'd been "in production," meaning he made the CDs, though Philip wasn't clear exactly what his uncle did, other than know lots of musicians. If asked, he joked, "It's music politics. I'm the *party organizer*." Philip had just last week overheard his mother describing him to his father as an "elderly gopher," and his father had shaken his head while agreeing. Lending the visit an air of illegality that Philip found thrilling, his mother had added, "He'd better not be bringing anything in from Jamaica." His father assured her his brother wouldn't. Philip loved hearing his father's moderate English accent spice up whenever he talked about Uncle Phil. He could almost picture his father as a boy, having fun.

Another thing his father said about his brother, sounding English as could be, was, "I can tell he's still fantastically lonely."

They walked a fair way, Uncle Phil wanting to "go past any people." So eager was he on this point that for a distance he carried Tommy and the basket at the same time, and when they arrived he was exhausted and he dropped both a bit abruptly. Tommy actually landed on his side and looked to Philip to see if he was supposed to cry.

Uncle Phil began immediately to unpack and assemble his kite. The breeze, he said, was brilliantly steady. Philip was sent up into the driftwood logs for a chunk of wood "the size of your own leg." When he returned with one, Uncle Phil moved them from the soft sand down to the hard-packed, low-tide sand. Tommy proudly dragged the shovel.

"Is the tide coming in?" asked Sasha, gazing out at the froth of breakers, its roar and roiling mist.

"Yes," Philip answered, trying to sound a warning, though he wasn't sure. The sand was cold and damp on his feet, and as hard as a floor. "And it comes in quickly. When I say it's time to move, we move."

But Sasha only wanted to hear that it was coming in. "Save the Queen! We can play Save the Queen!"

A game they played with tides, it involved a queen — a stick or a shell or moulded sand — around which you built a sand castle and fortress walls and outer walls and moats, all in an effort to keep the rising tide from getting in and drowning her. When the first surging flat tongues reached the moats and filled them, and then licked at the walls, which then began to crumble, the inevitable was upon you and so was the wonderful frenzy and panic to heap as much sand as fast as possible to shore up breaching walls. Last year at a gentler beach Sasha had actually lain down and used her body to plug a crumbling wall, screaming in hopeless joy, because the water just came and came, eventually breaking through and washing up to the sand-queen's feet — and down she came, dissolving — an outcome always known but always pretended against — otherwise there would be no reason to the game at all. Eventually they would simply give up and stand there breathing hard and, with open mouths and slack faces, stare at the dying.

"Just let me get my kite up and then we'll save the freaking queen."

The two smaller children were waiting for him. Still puffing from the walk, Uncle Phil sat down twice for a cigarette while he got his kite trick set up. From a Thermos he sipped what Philip knew to be gin. When little Tommy ran up to his uncle for a sip he was rebuffed with a laughing, "You don't want any of *this*, luv."

The kite was egg-shaped, with a Union Jack design on both sides. Against the monotones of sand and water, the colours of this design looked truly unnatural, bizarre even, and Philip fancied that high in the sky was the only place for it.

His uncle got the kite together and laid it on the ground under one foot for it really was quite breezy. He asked Philip to dig him a leg-sized hole and Philip shovelled until told to stop, about two feet down. Uncle Phil tied some clear fishing line to the long stake, placed it in the hole and buried it, with the invisible line protruding. He tied the fishing line to the kite-string handle. It was easy to get the kite airborne — cigarette in mouth, Uncle Phil looked almost athletic running five steps and tossing it aloft and playing out line — and soon the kite was sitting hard in the sky one hundred feet above them. At this point Uncle Phil let go of it completely.

The trick involved what you didn't see. With the hole smoothed over, what you did see was a kite and its string and its handle, suspended in mid-air, six feet off the ground, held by no one.

Uncle Phil twanged the fishing line, which was taut and holding invisibly well. He slapped sand from his hands. Staring at the eerie floating handle, not the soaring kite, he asked, "So what d'ya think?" He gazed up and down the beach for passersby, though there weren't any. "They'll think we brought our pet ghost," he said, and laughed lightly.

Sasha asked if they could play Save the Queen now.

It was Sasha who began constructing walls around Uncle Phil as he sat there on the sand admiring his kite trick. It was also Sasha who demanded that they had to "bury him all except for his head" when she decided that this king was way too big. Uncle Phil was fine with it, climbing stoically to lounging position in the long hole that was as deep as Philip could get it until the floor became solid water. His uncle shouted as he sat, declaring it "freaking ice" but loudly assuring himself it would warm up.

"You have to keep me in supplies," he told Philip, meaning his gin and cigarettes. He looked comical, padded collar of the hunting vest framing his jaws, hair weak in the breeze, cigarette bobbing as he talked. Classic disembodied head. Tommy enjoyed his task of leaning in with the Thermos cup and getting the drink in past the cigarette and into his uncle's mouth. Philip had to admit to pride not only at lighting a first cigarette but learning to do one in the wind. Uncle Phil was a good teacher. "The trick," he said, "is to cup your hand as close as you can to the flame without burning yourself. The thing is finding that one quarter inch."

Because this time the queen, or in this case king, was a person, the walls had to be higher, the moats deeper. Sasha and Tommy dug and pushed and moulded to keep their buried uncle from the calamity that roared ever closer, pounding out clouds of mist that turned a blue day cold, backed by ocean that filled the horizon and that your stomach knew never stopped.

Placing the latest cigarette in his uncle's lips, which reached out for it in a less-than-attractive way, Philip decided against telling him that his lips were turning purple. If the game ended now, with the wave surges not yet at the first moats, his brother and sister would be upset. Also Uncle Phil was still energetic with chatter, always about music. Because of the nearing surf, he had to shout. He really was a sight. Sasha had draped his head with a seaweed crown, a frond of which flipped windblown against a cheek.

". . . because it isn't English any more, it's Euro or brown. Now I *love* brown. Little Richard's my hero, mate. And I *had* my Ravi Shankar period. I mean we've never had music of our own 'less you want to include fucking *skiffle*." He laughed and Philip didn't know why, but his uncle was talking fast and not really noticing anyone. His teeth were actually chattering. "See you had Elvis translate black for us and these were the first invaders, which we digested and sent back as the Stones and Yardbirds and R and B whomevers, you catch my drift, but now you've sent us Britney and it makes me, it truly makes me hostile. All we can send you back this time is a big fucking bucket of *sweets*." He laughed again, and coughed. "Jesus, it's really cold in here, I don't know if . . ." Then he put his nose in the air to call out again comically, rolling the R, for "Brrrandy!", at which Tommy said "Yay!", ceased his scooping and, stepping carefully over the battlements, hurried in with the gin Thermos. Tommy's offering was unsteady and Uncle Phil shivered as he drank, and some dripped off his chin.

"I've met Sting. You know Sting, right?"

"No."

"Proof that *unbridled ambition* is all a bloke really truly needs, plus an instinct to go Hollywood at *the first ring of the freakin bell*. Sure he's *hand*some but . . ."

Uncle Phil wasn't talking to anyone but himself any more and Philip wished he would stop. An eagle was up in the snag behind them and at Philip's pointing Uncle Phil tried turning to look, but not really, and on he talked. Now three ravens — Philip's favourite bird — came to chase the eagle off and take its place in the trees, and though the ocean was loud he wanted his uncle to hear their croaks and screams and other sounds, especially the one exactly like a hugely amplified drop of water landing in a pool in the depths of a cave: *Plooink*. Sometimes ravens would make this sound back and forth, using different tones that seemed to mean something, or sounded intentionally funny, and Philip wanted to tell his uncle that at such times it was possible to believe that these birds carried the spirits of dead native elders who, it seemed, were comedians.

When a surging tongue from a big wave travelled up with a hiss, leapt two moats, and knocked through the first wall as if it weren't there, it was almost like this was a signal to Uncle Phil.

The only sign of his struggle was his head lifting, straining to rise above the sand.

"It's — it's *very cold actually*." He laughed out of a bed of weakness, and no hint of a smile. He seemed embarrassed. "I think I — Philip? Well, I don't think I can feel my . . . Actually, I think I have to — Phil?"

Uncle Phil's voice trailed off. He gritted his teeth and stretched his blue lips out away from them. His gums were grey. In the middle of that he appeared to go to sleep.

Philip could see that, barely halfway to the parking area, Sasha and Tommy had grown tired and had slowed to walking. A few people were moving about near the cars. Philip couldn't see their arms so he knew they couldn't see his either, so he stopped waving. He had tried one steady scream but it was nothing, he could barely hear it himself in the roar of the surf that was so close now.

At first they'd dug out Uncle Phil's arms and tried pulling, but it was immediately obvious that they weren't moving him at all. They'd dug some more, and got him clear to the waist, but still he wouldn't budge, and now Tommy had to kneel behind and plant himself and struggle to keep Uncle Phil's head propped out of the flats of wave that rushed in and submersed Tommy to his chest. Sasha fell prone to plug a breached wall, like two years ago, but this time there were no screams of delight, just hardly heard coughs of "Quick, quick." Tommy, big eyed and grim, knew his uncle wasn't playing and that all this panic had something to do with time. A bigger, quicker wave came in and Tommy lost his grip on his uncle's head and shoulders and Uncle Phil stayed under for a while because Philip was off feeling for the shovel. When the wave receded and his head reappeared and not being able to breathe didn't seem to have troubled him, that's when Sasha and Tommy saw it for real and started crying, and that's when Philip told them to run to the parking lot for help.

Philip knelt holding his uncle's head up as waves came in and went out. It was loud, and exhausting, and hard to know the true passing of time — maybe fifteen minutes went by before Tommy and Sasha reached the parking lot. By now the surges were up to Philip's chin, and his uncle's head was under half the time anyway, so finally Philip mumbled several words he couldn't hear himself mumble, let his uncle's head fall, and walked backwards, watching, to higher ground.

Philip knew he had miscalculated in some way. He had failed at something huge, something beyond him, and he wondered what his mother would say. He wondered how loud Aunt Sally would be, and when she would leave them and return to England. Would she stay with them tonight, or go to a motel? Tomorrow there would be no crispy bacon. His father no longer had a brother.

He stood ankle-deep and blank-faced as each wave hit, his uncle mounding the clear rushing water, like a boulder under the surface of a fast, broad river, a river that slowed to a stop and reversed before running over the boulder in the other direction. Each time the water receded and his uncle appeared, Philip looked for signs of revival, but nothing changed, except for the strand of seaweed rearranged at his uncle's neck and shoulders, and his thin hair which itself seemed like a pathetic variety of seaweed. Then a new wave hit, and then another, and Philip had to backstep to higher and higher beach until, deep carnival, all he could see of this relative was, just to the right, his kite trick.

FORMS IN WINTER

He should have worn a scarf. It's only late November but it's too cold, early cold that feels unwarranted, like punishment. It has hardened the soles of his shoes and the sidewalk jars his feet to the bone. It would feel warmer if there were snow. There's no one else out walking and his crisp footsteps echo almost comically — or is it a sinister sound, he can't tell which.

He is on his way to talk to the McGonnigals because he believes that, whatever one's own failings, and despite the possibility that one might make a bigger mess of things, it remains one's human duty to try to ease another's agony.

He picks his spots. The McGonnigals. Knowing so little about them he's aware that he might make that mess. He might get his nose broken again. But he's on his way to the McGonnigals, and he persists in this and in all needful things because of Andrew — Andy — fifteen years ago.

Of course there were those times, before Andy, when he didn't act and should have. One was on the south shore of the Island of Crete, when he was in his early twenties, in that small village — Aghia Ghalini. For a month he'd slept on a nearby beach with other, ever-changing travellers, and an outdoor taverna was their base for telling stories, and the long evening's retsina. Then at some point a waiter told them about the captive girl up the hill. In bits and pieces they got the story: a sixteen-year-old Australian girl who had lost her parents in a car accident had been sent to Greece to live with her next of kin, a Greek uncle, here in this village. From Sydney, she was a typical city teenager. At first she had been allowed out to the market, and to school, but she had been seen with a boy. Now her uncle kept her locked indoors. A rumour said he made her wear all black. Lately she had been sending notes — sometimes paper airplanes out the window! — begging for rescue, asking the Australian government for help. A waiter, Georges, had seen some of them himself. There was little sympathy for her in this village of arranged marriages and men-only tavernas, but Georges whispered that he was "her fren'" because she wasn't *really* Greek, and that people had heard her screaming, and in any case the uncle was "assahole." The girl's name was Cindy. Shaking his head, Georges added that Cindy "no eeffen speak a Greek."

The travellers talked about her. They were Canadians, Americans, a New Zealander. One night two Aussies drifted in and were outraged by the story. After much beer they walked the hill and pounded on the door of Cindy's prison and got into a shoving match with an older man and his sons. It was never determined if they got the right house. In any case the rest of them talked about what should be done. She was a minor, living with legal next of kin. Fate had landed her in a set of backward customs. The phrase "weird karma" had some of them nodding sagely.

He sometimes still wonders about Cindy. She'd be in her late forties now. He imagines her married, at a kitchen window peeling potatoes, long resigned to her fate. She speaks Greek now, of course. She's married to a man who treats her well enough because he knew from the start that she was different. She has not had children of her own.

But he didn't think about Cindy for years. Actually he didn't remember Cindy until after they found Andrew in the cement.

He's three blocks from the McGonnigals' street and he wonders if he's ever walked it, McRae Street, before. While his mission often takes him new places, the story is generally the same. He's going to ask them to hear their daughter's side of things and not to punish her. He's going to suggest that they ask *her* forgiveness. What he's going to remind the McGonnigals tonight is that their daughter is beautiful in every way.

He sometimes sees girls her age on street corners. Rarely, but he does, whenever he makes a point of searching for them. He'll spot one and pull up to the curb and roll his window down and she will step through the ghost of her own breath, closer. He feels doubly sorry for them in winter, when they dress just warmly enough not to freeze to death yet still show off their bodies. There is something not visually right about a girl in a tiny skirt and sheer pantyhose breathing white plumes of breath into the night air, something incongruous about a girl shivering and yet smelling of luscious, fruity perfume. When they approach his car window they are too out of it to care, or desperate for their next fix, or just stunned myopic —

but some study him clear-eyed to see if he'll be a danger. What they see in his eyes often does scare them, but of course it's not what they think. Only when he tells them, "Someone loves you very much. Please — *please* — go home," do they know what kind of danger he represents.

Sometimes he feels guilty for making them remember what they might be working so hard to forget. He does understand that they might in fact have no one at home who loves them. He knows their home might be the foulest cesspool of hurt, and he has just shouted another lie at them from his car window. But he likes to believe, has to believe, he did the right thing. It's crucial to be positive in these matters.

Otherwise why is he walking to the McGonnigals? He's on foot tonight because McCrae Street is only a mile from Glendale Apartments. He's lived in Glendale Apartments ever since they opened, because the building site is where they found his son, Andy. His wife, Andy's mother, never did join him here. They split rather quickly after Andy died. He learned this wasn't uncommon. It does feel quite wrong to stay together, as if the death somehow issued from the union itself. Indeed everything felt wrong for a time, as wrong as things can feel wrong, and their marriage blew apart like two dry leaves. He still thinks kindly of her and he senses she thinks the same of him, though years ago she moved off to a distant city and then, so he's heard, to another. So her method has been opposite to his. Here he stays, camped right on the spot. He even chose the northwest ground-floor corner unit, directly over the wall in the parking garage where they discovered him.

He turns onto McRae Street, and he decides his footfalls are neither comic nor sinister. They are the hard, nighttime sound of someone planting winter seeds.

He got his initial details about Rebecca McGonnigal — fourteen, Grade 9, brought home in a police cruiser, drunk — from the civilian dispatcher he befriended during Andy's disappearance. The rest of the information has been bled from the reluctant school counsellor who remains sympathetic because he had been Andy's counsellor, and who is consulted only rarely and whose name will be forever protected. The situation is that, since Rebecca's big night, her parents have grounded her, made her take a pregnancy test, have not let her return to school — eight days so far — and are even considering pulling up stakes and moving to another neighbourhood. The McGonnigals, says his source, are very religious. His source also informs him that Rebecca is an average student, moderately popular, and wryly but self-consciously witty. Her best friend is older, in Grade 10. His source doubts that she has ever kissed a boy, and suspects she may in fact be lesbian, or shamefully curious about that possibility.

None of this will he throw in the McGonnigals' faces. He will stay positive and keep to general principles. If given time he will tell them his own story. He hopes they will let Rebecca come out of her room to hear it.

On McRae Street the houses are noticeably more well-to-do and they appear somehow alien. But he decides that's him, and he's uncomfortable straying this far from Glendale Apartments. He feels it in his abdomen and he thinks it has to do with being on foot and drawing steadily away from where it is Andy hid and clung to those last days.

They used to live in a nice bungalow several blocks from where Glendale Apartments is now. He can see the attraction the building site had for Andy. For one, it was close to home should he decide to return. At the time, they were building the underground parking level, and the roofless pit of tall wooden wall-forms would keep him hidden at night. Apparently Andrew built at least one fire in there. Otherwise it's difficult to know what those long days and nights had been like for his son. He has never been able to find out if Andrew was alone or with others. A single muddy blue sleeping bag was found. He doesn't know if Andrew partied, or sat hugging his knees to think, or perhaps cry. He doesn't know if Andrew got stoned, or walked the streets in a steady, health-seeking way. He does know his son was angry because what his parents had done to him made no sense. But he likes to think that Andrew felt warmer staying close to home. It was January.

It began on January 1. Actually, December 31. Andrew had broken his New Year's Eve curfew, which was eleven o'clock. Though he's tried, he cannot remember if this particular time was his or his wife's idea, but the point is they hadn't told Andrew that one reason — the main reason? Wasn't it *the main reason?* — they chose eleven was to have him back to celebrate midnight with them. They had never given in, never negotiated matters of curfew, and he remembers Andrew's sullen shrug of agreement when they informed him. He thinks he suspected even then that Andrew was going to break it, that Andrew had already decided to break it, even while slouching out of the kitchen. He remembers Andrew's hair still wet, and tightly combed. And the slight smell of a hopeful cologne. He remembers too how small Andrew looked, and how young, and how it was still odd for them and somehow difficult to hear his newly deepened voice. He believes now that Andrew being small for his age made it easier for them to impose curfews that may have been more suited to someone a year or two younger. It's a mistake he's been admitting for many years. But he didn't admit it that night, when Andrew came in quiet as a mouse at two a.m. smelling of beer, guessing wrong that they'd be asleep. They grounded him indefinitely, banning all visits from friends. The more he fought against it, the more they dug in. They were conventional parents, and felt it vital to win this fight, if only to set the correct precedent. In the ensuing battle he and his wife had each other to bolster sagging spirits, assuage doubts. Andrew had no one. It's easy to see this now. In any case, two days later, Andrew left home. "Ran away." Their decent little Andrew. Or, Andy. Only since his death has he called him Andrew. It might be that, in the cement, his face stressed like that, he looked older. Maybe he's simply projecting an adult life onto the face, seeing an "Andrew" at a university. Though he'd have been long finished university by now.

Street lights cast a sheen of safety over these fine McRae Street homes, which sit as a portrait of the Canadian dream, a dream quieter, more modest than its louder cousin to the south. What we want is comfort, not wealth. Contentment, not fame. These houses do suggest contentment and comfort — he believes this is suburban architecture's unstated purpose — but he knows it is rarely the case inside.

The real dream — he will tell the McGonnigals — is to keep the child from chaos. The nightmare is to see the child enter chaos and be spun off into agony. To wake in horror is to know the child has been pushed there by your loving hands.

More than once in his walks he has come upon a new construction site and gone in. He has ripped good clothes on fences, but when the mood overtakes him nothing matters less than fences or clothes. The smell of turned earth, mud, and cold stone is so raw he can taste as well as smell it. The wood of the forms is sometimes pitchy, sometimes barely scented when it is old and battered from reuse. On the older forms the grey of cement coats the wood.

Sometimes it's night, but if it's day and there's a wall he'll get behind it and lie full out on the dirt, wet or not. He'll lie there and breathe. He feels the contour of the ground and the cold of it. He smells the sour richness of the raw, heaved earth. He opens his eyes to the dirt an inch away, notes the grit and particulate swirl and the surprising array of colour, ranging from yellow to black, and all the shades of brown in between. These are certainly some of the things Andy knew only too well during his last days, and at times it is overwhelmingly important that he knows these things too.

The McGonnigal house is one of the nicer ones. Emerging from the brick, white colonial half-pillars pretend to hold up a portico. He will stand out on the sidewalk a while and stare at it, into it. Sometimes he can read the quality of the light in the windows. Too often a TV's erratic blue pulse dominates, but sometimes in kitchens and other rooms there's light from which he can sense an emptiness and anger, or a desperate hope. Sometimes there's a peculiar creamy light that speaks of friendliness and ignorance.

They got the call the tenth day Andy had been gone. The police knew instantly whose body it was. He and his wife had been phoning incessantly for updates, and for leads from other cities. The search for the fourteen-year-old male — small for his age, blond, white sneakers, jeans, jean jacket with Redbone in leather stitches on the back — was national. But Andy never left the immediate area, never left the site of the future Glendale Apartments. The police explained that a worker pulling forms had discovered the body and — He interrupted to ask what "forms" meant. He learned that forms are plywood walls, built side by side a foot apart (in this case), into which cement is poured. A mould, really. He came to learn more about forms. After a week, when the cement has hardened, the forms are pried off, "pulled." Apparently it's a rough job, where men use pry bars and brute force and jump out of the way of falling sheets of cement-sodden plywood. Fingers get broken, faces are scraped, and hard hats fly. In winter, underground in a future parking garage, it's dark and bleakly cold.

One worker's job was made all the more bleak when he pulled a sheet of form away and there near the bottom, at the height of the worker's knees, instead of smooth new cement was fabric and flesh. Enough of Andy's face was showing that his father was asked to come and identify him while Andy was still in the wall. His mother didn't — couldn't — come.

He won't — he never does — go into much detail here, not even in his memory. Nor will he burden the McGonnigals with what they might construe to be scare tactics. He'll describe his son's pounded face simply by saying that his gut reaction at seeing it was relief that his son had obviously died quickly. He had arrived at the site already knowing his son was dead, and now he was learning that he hadn't suffered. So there was something positive to take from even this frigid cement underground.

In these later years, when something like humour finds its way to him, he can admit that the image of Andy's body set part in, part out of concrete resembled some art installations

he's since seen — modern art often uses that same clash of tex-
tures. Soft skin and denim and cement do not go.

No one could say why Andy was there before the cement got
poured, wedged between plywood forms a foot apart. The
autopsy showed he wasn't drunk. Nor had he been killed first
and dumped there. The word *suicide* was never ventured, for
an odd suicide it would've been, Andy jumping in even as he
saw the truck coming.

To this day he has no clue. As the cement began to fall, Andy
was either unconscious, or conscious, and either possibility
leads down ten unlit roads. He no longer belabours possibilities
because the point tonight and all nights is that his son left home
and needn't have, and here he is at the McGonnigals' door.

They are appropriately cautious. He gains entry because of
his standard shirt and tie and their assumption that he's here
officially when he mentions their daughter. Now it's up to him.
They lead him to the living room, Mrs. McGonnigal holding
his coat. They are so young. He expected Mrs. McGonnigal to
be bigger, but he's learned that people with steel principles
aren't always physically strong themselves. Her eyes tell him
that she feels most at home in a church. She wears a sweater of
lemon and rose, quenching fruit colours that deny this wintry
night. Big and smooth and mulish, Mr. McGonnigal wears a
fixed, mindless smile, and a two-piece Nike track suit though
his hair is in no way mussed. This will be hard.

Everybody takes a seat. He sits in the easy chair that matches
their couch, where the McGonnigals perch side by side. Mr.
McGonnigal points the remote at the TV but pauses a moment
before turning off a nature show, a cheetah gazing into the
vista from a rock outcrop, the odd feline's body lithe and bony
and in these ways resembling the antelope it is built to catch.

He asks them, "Might Rebecca be included in this?"

"No, that's fine," Mrs. McGonnigal says, not bothering to ask what it is her daughter won't be included in. Her husband sits very still, eyeing him and not blinking.

He doesn't know how long they will let him stay. They wait, watching him with judgement and anger and hope conjoined, and in their eyes he sees how their week has gone and how their life is laid out.

"You have a beautiful, very precious daughter," he begins, and from the way they nod in clear-eyed agreement, so certain that what he's just said is true, he wonders again why he doesn't just stand and leave, exactly now.

Beneficent

THE BEAST WATERS HIS GARDEN
OF A SUMMER'S EVE

<Keymaster Transcription Service @ 5 dollars per typescript page. Request specs: 12 point, no quotation marks, italics as per inflection>

Hello?

Okay, I know it's really early but —

Rich?

— I really have to talk.

Jesus **<And indistinguishable>** Christ.

Sorry, I waited as long as I could.

Time is it?

I think it's maybe —

Jesus, it's six-thirty. What's —

Forgot, sorry, it's seven-thirty here. I waited all I could wait. Man, I really blew it, I pulled an unbelievable stupid one and I need you to do something for me. I've been up all night.

What happened?

I still can't believe what I did.

What did you do, Rich? You get fired again?

Vice-presidents don't get fired. I don't get fired. When I didn't make partner, I left. You've *never* under —

Okay, right, right.

Well you never have.

You and Carol okay? You didn't, ah . . .

No, I didn't. We —

Well, that's good.

Violence just isn't in me any more.

That's good.

I mean we're okay and we're not okay, it's nothing like that, not of that realm, just — Somehow it's bigger. It's really, really strange. Odd. Wide as the sky. Getting wider even as we speak.

What's happened?

Okay, you know how we might be Jewish?

I thought it turned out we weren't.

No, we're Jewish. We're a quarter Jewish. Mom's half Jewish.

Well, no, it turned out the guy came from France.

No, our great-grandfather came from Alsace, which was in Germany at the time, and he had a German name.

Jesus, Rich, what did you do? It's six in the morning.

His name was Michel, pronounced *My*-kell, that throat-clearing Hebrew thing, which can only mean Jewish in that part of the world —

Okay, we'll be Jewish.

Well no we really are — a quarter Jewish — and anyway I've been telling the kids that.

Okay. So?

So it's sort of been a neat joke lately, all of us being part Jewish, because it's kind of cool, kind of a —

You like the genius thing, I know.

Well, the persecution thing too, all of it. But, yeah, the *genius* thing, the *artistic* thing, just the general —

Jerry *Lewis* thing.

Fine. **<Or profanity>**

So anyway?

In fact just last week at this party here these friends of Carol's sort of gave me a bar mitzvah. They planned it. The woman, Wendy, is hard-core Jewish and knows all these Yiddish songs and sat me in a chair in the centre of the room and was dancing around me, singing, while she made me wear this fake yarmelke with these sideburn curls hanging from it, and bob my head while I pretended to read this fake book. Stuff like that, it was a hoot.

So?

Anyway I've been up all night, haven't slept. I'm babbling a bit but —

You still with that therapist? You said looks like —

Marilyn Monroe's sister. No.

Is it about any —

This is nothing like that. It's not the compulsive thing, which is controlled, which is very much under control. She was a fraud by the way and I'm suing her — I know how I raved about her for a while there. But she *was* good at drugs and now I take a little beige pill every morning and it works and even if I miss a day I don't even notice. So I'm better. It's not that. I'm not a nut. This is real, and it is very unfortunate. I'm worried about my kids, my house, my *career*. So don't make psychiatric jokes, all right?

I just needed some context. You have a history. I have to ask questions. I've never thought you were a nut. I've always just thought — Well, we've talked about this.

No, what? What have you always thought?

You know, that you're always, I don't know, playing roles. That. Not being yourself. Not being straightforward.

Well, touché, sure. Though I don't agree.

Not "touché," I'm not trying to win anything here. I'm just saying what I think. It's not a competition.

Okay. You're right. But —

Just a sec, my water's whistling.

— calling someone for help at seven in the morning, I don't know how much more "straightforward" you can get. I've never been more direct. What could *be* more direct. So whatever you say . . . Anyway even though it started this mess, it's been fun lately, the Jewish thing. I've been using words like "mensch" and "schlong" around the kids and stuff like that and —

I'm back. Coffee.

    — I talk in a loud Jewish accent sometimes, like: "YOU CALL THIS A BAD STEAK? IT'S GOOD. *GOOD.*"

Sounds like a loud New York accent.

Well, whatever. They were good steaks.

Rich.

What.

What did you do?

Okay, we're just back from the beach, right?

Okay.

Qualicum, right? Where we go? We were there two weeks, and, the thing is, I didn't shave the whole time. The whole time.

Jesus, Rich —

It's part of the deal here, it's the, it's the heart of the story.

Okay.

Okay, well, yesterday I shaved. I had quite a beard going, really thick, it surprised me. I had to go out and buy a razor and foam. The gel. Haven't done that in years. But my electric couldn't hack through it.

Rich. What did you do?

I shaved, but in the middle of shaving I did this little joke, this little thing where I left a Hitler moustache on, right?

You have a Hitler moustache?

For a while I did, yes. I had a Hitler moustache and I walked around the house, you know, pretending nothing was different, just walking around — Carol's in there cooking dinner and on the phone, and Richard's there on the computer, and Jennifer's down watching the tube — right?

Okay.

So I just wandered around kind of leaning my head into their, you know, various activities, let them catch on to my joke at random and be delighted and outraged, etcetera, by "Well, here's Dad with a Hitler moustache."

Did they think it was funny?

Do you think it's funny?

I thought it was funny when John Cleese did it.

Touché.

Actually he just had his finger curled there, his knuckle. It was mostly his goose step that was great.

I'm the first to admit I force things. Which was exactly the case. But, you know, I'm playful. You'd think that seeing their lawyer vice-president father fooling around with a Hitler moustache, their *Jewish* vice-president father, you'd figure they'd, you know, I don't know . . . "laugh."

You can't predict these things.

You *really* can't.

So, Rich?

Yeah.

That's not your problem, is it? That they didn't laugh?

Not exactly.

It's really not a six-in-the-morning problem.

It gets bigger.

Good. I mean —

No, that's fine. And here it comes. But them not reacting to my little moustache caused the whole thing, right? It was the catalyst. It was why —

They didn't laugh at all? It's actually pretty funny that you'd do that. I like it that your little things are getting weirder. I would have laughed. I'm laughing now.

Well, how funny it was is now moot.

What'd they do? Just stare?

They all had their different thing. Carol's, I think, was the worst one, was the one that made me go and — But she came last. First, Jennifer just said, "Eeeeuuu." That's it. And turned back to her TV show. I basically had to stick my face in the way of her TV show so she'd see it at all. But that was it: "Eeeeuuu." Then back to *Canadian Idol*. Entranced. White people from Richmond Hill singing scat. Jennifer is enraptured, like it's her own future, her own stardom, tied up in this show. I think she thinks she can sing.

Well, she *can* sing. Have you ever —

She's not even blinking at these showy creeps, and for me it's: "Eeeeuuu." Also, I don't know, I actually think it's . . .

What.

I think it's the only thing Jennifer has said to me in a week or two, but that's a different issue altogether.

She's fifteen now right?

Fifteen.

There you go. It's really not you.

I suppose not.

So Carol made you do something?

Well, first there was Richard.

Right. Richard's at the computer.

At the computer, where he always is. Playing his six-things-at-once: you know, some on-line blasting game, plus talking to his friends a mile a minute, plus downloading songs, probably some porn going on in there somewhere, it just boggles me why —

Robbie's pretty much the same way, I know the deal.

Exactly. And how they type so fast, faster than secretaries, it's ten fingers at once, it sounds like "*scrabble*," and when you read it you see there's no spelling, no capitals, no punctuation, hardly even words. I mean it's initials, acronyms, it's meaningless.

Well, to us.

No it's meaningless. What are they talking about? "Hey Ray, it's Richard, what are you doing?" When obviously Ray is sitting on his ass typing like secretaries, just like Richard.

"Whacha doin' later, Ray?" When what they're doing later is what they're doing now. It pisses me off, it really does. Everything either rocks or it sucks and it's all infinitesimal *crap*, I'm sorry.

You want them to be discussing world politics. Well, me too.

Or at least "What about that ass on Sheila." Even that.

Right.

Or even better, "Let's go down to 7-11 and check *out* that ass on Sheila." You know, engage in some non-screen activity.

Thing is, I think girls are in on the chat lots of the time. They're actually talking to girls, or at least typing with girls, so they can't very well, you know . . .

See their actual ass.

No, I mean *talk* about their actual — Anyway, look, so you stuck your moustache in front of Richard?

I did.

And.

And Richard actually stopped everything. It was actually very dramatic. He saw my face. He stopped typing. He pulled his hands away. Though his elbows were still cocked. He looked at me for quite a long time, and then his face blossomed with a giant sneer.

Strike two. So Carol was strike three.

Well, Richard said something to me. It's made me think.

What.

I didn't think about it right when he said it, I thought about it after. Quite a bit, actually.

Okay, let me go top up my coffee. I'm just going to put my phone down. Five seconds.

What he said was, "What are *you* making?" That's what he said. I realize that probably I have to —

I'm back. What?

I have to explain a little bit.

I'm sort of waiting for you to do that, Rich.

No, about Richard and what he said to me.

Sure. All right.

See, the thing is, about a month ago I believe I really scared him. He probably would never admit it, but I really scared him.

What did you do?

What I did was this. I told him I was going to tell him the most valuable thing he could ever possibly hear during this life on planet Earth, and then I went ahead and told him.

Excellent. Well done.

Actually, I'm serious.

You going to tell me too, or is it secret?

Well, it's what they call self-secret, it's —

What who calls?

You know, wise men. Self-secret means it's there for everybody but nobody hears it because of the *nature* of the secret. The utter *size* of the secret.

Okay. Hit me.

What I told him is, "Richard, I'm going to tell you the best thing and the worst thing you're ever going to hear." We were actually into a formal father-and-son talk. I had called him away from the computer and outside onto the lawn. He was so impatient he could hardly bear it. He could not look me in the eye. But I had to get him away from that influence.

I could never do anything remotely like that with Robbie.

Well, I admit it was a little bit forced, but it was time. And I told him. I figured that, at the very least, even if he didn't act on it, I'd know he was exposed to the truth and I'd done my duty.

So you told him what?

I said to him: The best thing you'll ever be told is this. That every moment, every second you are alive, *you can make your self*.

Okay, sure.

You know the concept.

Sure. It's not all that —

Fairly standard, I know, but wait. What I said next, and the part that pissed him off and scared him and made him say what he said to me about my Hitler moustache, was this: I also said to him: The *worst* thing you'll ever hear on this planet, is that, every moment, every second you are alive, you *are* making your self.

Okay.

You know? You can't *not* make yourself?

I guess, sure.

No, it's heavy. It's the big damnation thing in its essence, it really is. It says that every second you're being lazy or even just spacing out, you are *making* yourself into that. Every —

But it's not like it isn't reversib —

Every second you are either bettering yourself or damning yourself. That's what I told him and that's what he understood. It's been eating at him for a month, I think. Or, same thing, he's been trying to forget what he heard. He's been at the computer non-stop. Or sleeping. He won't even look at me. Or he's bolting out the door to the Sev for a slurpee, or eating way too much and too fast, or flicking through the TV like he's running from something, it's really, he's extremely scared by this notion —

Rich? I think possibly you're reading into this a little bit, maybe.

Maybe, but anyway, this is what he says to me, while he's sneering. He sees the moustache, and me all smiley, and he says: "What are *you* making?"

What did you say?

I said, "Touché." That's all. I didn't really think about it much till later. He said it more like, "Whatta *you* makin'?" Like Joey, in *Friends*. It pisses me off. Richard has a hefty IQ on him and he talks like that. They all do.

Is that your problem, that you think you're making yourself into something bad?

No, that's not what I'm talking about here. It was mostly Carol.

Right. Carol's turn.

I go to show Carol next, she's in the kitchen, on the phone. Sitting on that stool by the counter? You know that stool?

Yup.

Facing the doorway. So I stand there, framed in the doorway. Just sort of doing nothing. She glances up, nothing registers, goes back into gossip mode. It's her mother. They could talk for an hour choosing a shower curtain. So I do a little pose to get her to look again. She doesn't. So I go, "Ahem," and she looks at me, right into my eyes, and I rub my chin — you know, that, "I've just shaved and it was a nice, close shave" thing on my chin. You see up at the beach I didn't shave for two weeks so —

So it made sense to do that.

I stand there doing the chin rub, really exaggerated, and smiling, and she's looking right at me, maybe eight feet away and — guess what?

She hated it. She shot you a look of hate.

No.

I don't know. Her jaw dropped? She got scared?

No.

So what did she do?

Nothing.

What do you mean?

She didn't even notice it. Didn't even see it.

Really?

I have pretty dark hair, right?

Sure. <**Or profanity**>

I mean, almost black.

Yes, Rich, it's still pretty much dark.

And my skin is pretty white, right?

Our people have been long away from the sun of the holy land and would not easily be taken for Semites, no.

Touché. But even after two weeks at the beach. I have this pale skin, and black hair, which means any Hitler moustache I decide to grow on my face is going to be an extremely notice-able, let me say *successful*, Hitler moustache.

You'd think.

It was. It was *glaring*. But she just stared at me, right at me, right at my face, and didn't see it.

Funny.

No. Let me put it another way: she saw me with a Hitler moustache, and *she didn't see anything different about me.*

Ah, right. I getcha.

Get it?

I get how in the wee hours you could get a bit symbolic with that and see it as a problem.

That's not the problem.

That's still not the problem?

It's maybe a problem with me and Carol, and it's maybe a problem for me to deal with, but it's not why I called you.

Look, Rich, my phone here is beeping.

That what that is?

The battery's going to cut out in a minute, less than a minute. Here's a choice: I'll call you back in five hours, all rested and cheerful. Or I go downstairs to my regular phone and we continue this. You want to continue this?

Go to the other phone.

Okay. I'm walking.

Because I have a favour to ask.

Okay . . .

Good. Thanks.

No, I mean I'm on my way down the stairs.

Thanks.

No, honey, it's Rich, it's okay.

What?

That was Leslie. We woke her up. Okay, I'm here. Here. Can you hear me?

Yes.

Okay, I'll hang up this one. Can you still hear me?

You know my garden, right?

I know your garden.

It's where I went after Carol didn't notice.

You doing all those tomatoes again this year?

And lots of other stuff. Trying fennel. That fish soup you really liked?

It was okay.

No you loved it. It's that almost-licorice taste in it. Fennel. The bulbs in the grocery store cost almost five bucks each to buy. So I'm growing fennel. And tons of lavender. It's Carol's, actually, she wants to do these silk pillows, these miniature silk pillows filled with dried lavender, it's supposed to help you sleep, you put it near your nose in bed. It's a what's-her-name, the insider-trading trouble-lady —

Martha Stewart.

— it's a Martha Stewart thing, Carol wants to give one to every-body for Christmas presents this year. You guys are getting one.

For Hanukkah?

Right. Anyway there's a field of lavender this year, and it's me who waters it. It's what I like to do, water my garden.

I've seen you stand there.

Always handheld. Whenever I'm really angry or need space or hungover, I just —

You're off the wagon, Rich?

It's not a problem. Once in a while.

You sure?

I'd tell you if it was.

The first step is telling yourself.

My only addiction these days is I water my garden. Carol has to call me in for dinner. Sometimes I overwater. I told her it feels like nurturing, like I can feel the plants just drinking it up, and being sort of thankful, it's a bounteous feeling I get. Once I told Carol it was my only opportunity to feel as nurturing as a woman and she asked if I pictured the water coming out my breasts.

I like Carol.

She's good, sometimes she's good. Anyway, I take my little failed-moustache problem with me out to the garden and water it. I'm standing there watering the lavender, and then I'm in the tomatoes, nurturing away, and then I switch hoses and move to the flowers, and next I'm at the fence surrounded by beans. Right?

I'm picturing you with this weird smile and water coming out your breasts and it's too early in the morning for this.

Fine.

I'm going to be blunt and ask you to get to the point, and then I will do whatever it is you ask me to, Rich.

Fine. Here it is. I'm watering the beans. I'm watering the beans for a long time. Thing is, I've long stopped thinking about the beach, and shaving, and "Eeeuuu" and what I might be "making of myself," and being invisible to Carol. I'm just watering beans and feeling pretty much okay now, because the beans are soaking it up and thanking me. And along come Heather and Tom Lavoie, next-door neighbours, out for their walk.

Okay. Yeah?

Get it?

Get what.

We talked.

Yeah?

I'm watering my garden. We talk over the fence. But things feel very weird. Guess why.

Oh. Jesus.

See?

You talked with your neighbours with your Hitler moustache on?

Even *I* forgot I had a Hitler moustache. In the end even *I* didn't notice.

Holy.

Yes. I'm watering. We chat but not long. Suspiciously not long. They said they were tired or something from their walk but in retrospect I saw that they basically ran from me.

Must have been quite something for them.

Indeed. The Beast out watering his garden of a summer's evening.

They didn't say anything directly?

Nope.

But for sure they saw it?

Yup.

But Carol didn't.

No, they saw it. They ran. And then you can bet they talked about it all night.

You'd think they'd make a joke. You know, to acknowledge yours. You'd think friends would say something.

Well they aren't friends, they're neighbours. The other thing is, they didn't see it as a joke.

How do you know?

They ran away from me.

Right.

It gets worse. It wasn't just them. I kept watering. I didn't get it yet. A few others crawled by in cars and we waved. The MacCarthys came by with their dog and we talked. One car contained a man name of Wolf Heisl. Wolf Heisl — what the hell did *he* think? But then, the *grand fucking finale*, Richard's drama teacher with two bags of groceries. I mean, he was ten feet away. We only ever say hi — we said hi. But you should have seen the look on his face. It was this look that, that, finally made me remember. What was on my face, out there in public.

Man.

Do you know what Richard's drama teacher's name is?

No.

Joel *Green*berg.

Oooo.

Greenberg.

Ouch.

I've been up all night.

I guess I can see why.

Do you?

Neighbours, teachers, it's embarrassing.

It's more than that, man. It's more than that.

Ouch. So what did you want me to do?

A man can be a nut in our neighbourhood, and nobody says a thing.

It's polite times.

A man could be *on fire*, and people would just say hi.

Right.

Hitler could be *living on our street*, and nobody would say a thing.

You're pretty much right.

Our politicians are conducting evil — *evil* — and everyone knows it, deep down, but no one *says anything*.

Well, maybe, but you need some sleep, brother.

No one laughed. Ergo, they thought I was serious. They thought *I* thought I was Adolf Hitler. And nobody said a thing. As far as they are concerned, Hitler lives on their street and nobody's saying anything. A man named Greenberg didn't scream at me, didn't try to get at me and rip my face off.

I see your point but you might be getting a bit extreme with —

Well, I've been up all night.

Things won't seem so bad after you sleep a bit. They really won't. You might even see some hu —

But they *are* saying something. All I can picture are my neighbours calling each other, maybe even organizing a meeting, all of them talking about me, about me wanting to be Hitler and what are they going to do about it, all my kids' teachers and Carol's yoga friends and checkout girls and —

You have to calm down a bit, man.

— calling the police, and my work, calling my *partners*, can you imagine that? Can you picture that? I mean I'm not the only Jew in our firm, right? It's really quite something this time, I really can't —

Rich?

— see a way out of this one. I mean I'm just waiting for the eggs to start hitting the house, the people with fucking *torches* outside, painting, you know, a pink star or something on our door.

Rich?

Yeah.

Hitler's door didn't get painted. He did the painting.

Well, there's my first point. Hitler's alive and in the neighbourhood and nobody's doing anything about it.

Well, why don't you organize a mob and go get him.

Okay, sure, touché, mock me here.

You really need some sleep. Then you need to make a couple
of calls.

Calls.

Call up the people who saw you and explain to them. No
harm done. But get some sleep first. You're a maniac right now
and you'll scare them.

What the hell do I say to them?

Just explain what happened. Tell them what you told me.

Yeah, right.

Why not?

I tell them I had a Hitler moustache on purpose?

Well, that much they already know, Rich. You're just clarify-
ing for them that you had no, you know, evil intent. You were
playing a joke.

I tell a man named Greenberg I was playing a joke? Having a little, what, Hitler-fest?

Isn't that what you were doing?

It was a private, family thing.

Okay Rich, whatever. It's an idea. Telling the truth is an idea. I didn't want to say this, but being straight with people isn't your forte, never has been, and maybe it'll hurt to work at it, but there might be no other way this time. Either that or, yes, chances are people will talk a bit. Not like what you're imagining, but for sure people are going to, you know, marvel over it. Who wouldn't?

You're right but . . . I had another idea. A favour.

Okay, shoot. I love you, but my ear is getting sore. And I need to go for a walk. Then start work.

You still write at home?

Always.

You working on that, what, that historical novel still?

That and a play.

Stories?

Not lately.

Well, that's my idea. My favour to ask you.

Yeah?

You've always been the creative one, right?

Okay, sure.

I mean from day one.

I guess. So?

So tell me what to say. Create something for me.

Rich, that isn't what —

Write a story about this.

Hmm. I'm not sure I get —

It's even a good *idea* for a story.

It's not my kind of story, Rich. I wouldn't have a clue what —

Well, *that's* what I want you to do.

Why?

It'll solve everything.

How?

Well, lots of people read your stuff. I mean I talk to —

They really don't.

I talk to people every day who ask, "What's your brother writing now?" and "I sure loved his last one," and —

Rich. Hardly anyone reads my stuff. Seriously.

I know you don't make a dime but, no, they really do. And they will. When even one neighbour reads the story, or even *hears* you did a story about a Hitler moustache, word will get around and they'll know it's about me and I'll be absolved.

This is supremely confused on your part.

It's a good story. It'll work.

Why don't you just tell them yourself?

Because in the story I'll come off better.

How so?

Well, in your story I'll be conducting an experiment about, about "modern Jews," you know, in North America, and neighbourhood attitudes, and what people would do, or more to the point wouldn't do, if they encountered Adolf Hitler. It's a noble experiment I'm doing.

You want me to make all that up?

Well, I was sort of doing that.

You weren't remotely doing that.

In an after-the-fact way, I sort of was. But in your story, that's what I'm doing, and everyone's fears are quelled, and I even come off as sort of — I don't know — "interesting." "Brave," in fact. It's a risky thing to do.

What a lawyer.

I'm taking that as a compliment.

Rich, c'mon, it's a dumb idea and I'm really not going to do it.

Fine. <**Possibly profanity**> Please.

I have to add that this is maybe the most indirect —

I didn't want to remind you, but I will, of those times back in the not-so-good old days when you were having some problems meeting your, you know —

You paid my rent a few times, I'm eternally grateful, I paid you back. This is years ago, Rich. And you keep reminding me.

And now I'm asking you for the return favour.

I've never once mentioned that you charged me interest, Rich. Rich: you charged me interest.

That's not an abnormal thing. If you find it so, I apologize.

And you own twenty percent of everything I will *ever make*.

It's a contract we signed. It's business.

Not even an agent charges that. I'm your brother.

I bailed you out.

Some rent money. Years ago. Ratty little *basement suite*.
\<inaudible profanities\>

Where would you be now if I hadn't?

Anyway — Rich? — it's not my kind of story. Lacks a certain
ring of truth.

You're kidding.

And there's no, no punchline to it. There's no meaning. Not
my style.

Maybe he encounters the mob and . . . and talks them down.
I don't know, *make it up*. You're a fiction writer. You lie all the
time.

Actually I don't.

What's the big deal? I'm asking you a favour. I'm worried here.

I don't think it'll work.

It'll be hard-hitting. It'll be entertaining.

I think you should just tell the truth.

I can't! How?

I think the truth would make a better story. It might be kind of funny. Maybe even a little touching. Human, anyway.

I disagree.

I'm the writer.

Well, I'm a strategist.

That's for sure.

And I'm extremely good at it.

In that case I'm going to ask you what Richard asked you: what are you making?

Oh, come on.

Maybe you need some help making your self.

What do you mean?

Rich? I'm having an idea.

What.

You ever hear the concept, "holding a mirror up to nature?" It was Shakespeare.

No.

You know how I always used to carry that little tape recorder with me? For dialogue? Tape conversations?

No, but sure.

Well, I found it so helpful, I've been taping my phone calls. For a couple of years now.

What? Even this one?

It comes on automatically. Sometimes I review the tapes. It helps me with cadence and stuff. New expressions. And people say the most revealing things about themselves, but always in the most . . . indirect ways.

I'm sure they do. Fascinating.

Actually, I'm serious, Rich.

About what.

About the truth. About how the story is the conversation we've been having.

No way.

Well, "way." Maybe it's a story.

I'm a lawyer. I won't let it happen.

Ah, who gives a shit.

You're serious.

Let's just tell the truth.

Don't please. **<Profanities shouted away from the receiver>**

It'll solve both your problems. You explain yourself to everyone, and you tell the truth for a change. Start making yourself.

I don't think so. Don't, please.

Everything you've said, everything you will say next, is the truth. It's just — a mirror.

I don't think so.

The truth is all it can possibly be.

Turn it off.

I'll be doing it out of love. It'll be medicine. For your family. I'm actually serious, Rich.

I'm on the verge of hanging up.

Well, that'll be punctuation, won't it?

You're in it too.

Yes! It'll be cleansing!

You're a weirdo. You've always been a weirdo. *You're* the weirdo.

C'mon, why not.

I'll come off like an asshole.

You really won't. People will see you clearly and they'll understand.

No, they won't.

It'll be — it'll be self-secret.

You're the asshole now.

Well, I'll be exposing myself too.

Jesus, no.

We'll do it together. It'll be humbling for both of us. It's my career, and it really isn't that good a story.

No way.

We're already doing it. We're doing it now. It's almost done! This is the easiest story, I'm not even typing! This is the — **<Inaudible words and laughter>**

You're laughing at me!

I'm not! **<laughter>** I am!

I'm going to hang up.

You're right, we're always making ourselves!

I'm hanging up.

It's a story. It might even work. I can feel it working.

It's not a story.

That's never for the writer to judge.

I'm not the — I don't know what to do.

Why don't you get some sleep?

That's not what I *mean*.

Rich?

What.

Trust me. Everyone will know exactly what you mean.

< **FREEDOM** >

Wa comes breathless to the door but stops. The glass door is a black mirror and he has surprised himself again. Here he is: Wa. His eyes are not blue but he is handsome as hell. He gives himself the wink of Downey Jr., the one that says, *J'arrive.*

Wa's dreams are all coming true. America is *vachement* cool, at least Des Moines. It is so cool that, right beside this pawnstore (where he missed his beanbag chair by a week, the lady said) is a gunshop. Paris didn't have gunshops or pawnstores, not like this, with guns right next to — sometimes — beanbag chairs.

Wa has his paper in his pocket. He has waited his weeks while they check him out. He can picture the FBI googling him bigtime, can see a row of them at their computer screens with his face on it, or one with his hollow skull in glowing green bars like an empty birdcage turning slowly around. They'll know he's spelt "Roi," meaning king, even though you just say

"Wa." (Here in America — his mother laughs and points at him — they'll say *Roy*.) The FBI probably know his shoe size. And they will know Wa was three when he moved to Paris with his mother but that he has always been *Americain* even though — as everyone tells him — he has a shits way of talking. (You can't speak French *or* English, his mother laughs, pointing when he tries to speak something.) The FBI know every city in Europe she modelled in and how she was rich but sure isn't now, and they'll know when she got out of the skinny-clinic, though she still paints her nails with one thin line of nail polish because one line alone isn't fat, and he bets they track all her monsterfag boyfriends, especially that short one with the carrot breath who tried to poke him when he was twelve and who probably winces still and covers his *petit pois* even at the thought of Wa, and for sure they know how his *crazyfou* ideas got him kicked out of schools until there weren't any American ones left so he isn't the best reader in the world — if that's a crime, to not read, fuck them. But, *merde*, maybe they also know how on his eighteenth he sort of spent some hours in jail in Lyons after they found him on the bathroom floor *à la gare*, no shirt, he'll never drink *pastis* again, but come on, *ce n'est pas possible*, they can't not let him have a gun because of that.

Wa reads the window, the one word he knows: GUNS. He has already decided where it will go in his pants. He's seen how you stuff it in the front, but he's also seen the gun go off — once right in the meatpipe, and once, in a comedy western, in the cowboy boot. The main thing is to never have the gun barrel near veins. Wa's main fear is bleeding to death. To just drain like that. When you're stabbed or shot *comme ça* it doesn't hurt much and you're awake, just draining. You see it so much: the buddycop runs up and cradles your head, and you look up and say what's important. You feel like a hose is running inside but there's no handle to turn off — *Jesus merde* that freaks him out. In fact he saw a RealTV on it, on emergency rooms, a poor *mec* just sitting there and the nurse sees him turn white and she knows it's internal bleeding, meaning the hose is on inside and they're calling your loved ones in, who see your skin as white as your eyes and they cry, and all you feel is this deep-hose on, and you have no muscles left as everyone watches you drain and waits for you to say what's important.

So Wa's gun is going to be stuffed in the back of his belt, pointing at the least veins he can think of, the bum.

He stands at the glass door and takes his paper from his pocket, checks his face, and wonders if the FBI know he's gained fourteen-and-a-half since coming to America and that his new face is bigger than in his passport. They won't know his mother has yelled at him every time he steps on the scale. The thing with Paris is, the food costs too much. The thing with America is, MacDonald has two-cheeseburger events, and how can you *exactly* walk by that, even though your mother says all the salt they use makes you retain water in your fat cells? (It is hard for her to *say* "fat cells," so you know she is afraid for you.)

But how can you resist the treasure here, *Jesus merde*. Wa isn't sure, but he thinks America gives things away. He has passed signs outside two restaurants, signs with American flags on them that say, Wa is pretty sure, free fries. That's the word "free" up there, and he knows "fries," and these are restaurants across the same street from each other and this place is *vachement incroyable*. Not even his mother will be able to go skinny here.

So Wa loves America, Des Moines anyway. He has two hundred channels and the taxi drivers are nice, unlike Paris where they won't talk to him because of his shits French, unless they're Alergian. Here, he can speak his shits English and they ask him where he's from. He says "Par*ees*" and they love it, even though one turfed him from the taxi because of Iraq, the country that's on one hundred of the two hundred channels. From other taxi drivers he hears Saddam jokes and towel-head jokes and some ask him, Why you in Des Moines? He doesn't know how to say that his mother, a Jewish–Puerto Rican ex-model, is chasing a *mec* she married who owes her a truckful of money, and she's reduced to prostitution (she cries and laughs on the phone to a boyfriend in Paris about this, though Wa thinks she is joking), so Wa just tells them he's in Des Moines to buy a beanbag chair and a gun and he nods and winks his Travolta-in-*Pulp-Fiction*. Sometimes they wait when he goes into Mac-Donald for his burgers and sometimes they disappear. The thing is, America isn't fast. There's line-ups for your burgers. He has a wait-for-your-gun paper in his pocket, and he is waiting for a beanbag chair in the pawnstore. He's phoned malls in the skirts and can't find one. He's never really sat in one but he knows how beanbags feel and he's seen in teenflicks how the idea is that they fit your lazy teenage body. As of a few months ago Wa's no longer a teenager, but his plan is to get his beanbag chair, turn on his TV, take some steps back, then run to it and jump. If he lands like he's already sitting flat like in Frasier's dad's La-Z-Boy, that's how he'll stay. If he lands like in a Malkovich-in-a-powdered-wig straight wooden chair, that's how he'll sit. And it will fit him no matter how fat he gets. It'll fit his ass even with a gun in his belt back there. If the gun goes off and shoots into his beanbag chair, *pas problem*, a group of beans is *complètement* without veins.

Wa pushes open the door to the gunshop and the electronic song greets him like it has every day for weeks, but today is the day on his paper. Whenever he comes to look at his gun, one of the waiters here talks to him and one of them doesn't. Wa has learned that in America, you don't shake everybody's hand when you see them. He's also learned you don't piss in a park even if you turn your back. So he doesn't stick out his hand, just keeps it in his pocket, which in Paris would mean you are angry. Behind the counter today is the wrong waiter, the guy who's Wa's height so they are *exactement* eye to eye, and he thinks Wa is stupid, and Wa believes also that with his Jewish–Puerto Rican skin, plus a tan from eating on McPatios, he's as dark as a towel-head and it's a problem for this guy. In Paris lots of Algerians smile at him and even talk to him in their shits language.

Over his gun, which sits under the glass, Wa places his paper. His mother helped him with it. She was surprised to see it, but then she said their neighbourhood isn't the best and a gun would be *très très bizarre et chic*. She wants to keep it in her night table, but Wa knows she'll forget and he can have it for his pants.

The *mec* who doesn't like him is very eye to eye now and Wa smoothes the paper on the glass with his hands that are nervous and damp. The *mec*, who has a tightcap and grand moustache like the Hulkster, does not speak. He does not speak for so long, Wa knows it's rude. He wants to call the guy a *cont*, because his mother told him it's the worst word here, which is funny, since in Paris everyone's a *cont*, mothers tell their daughters to *arrête tes conneries*. He wonders if Sean Connery knows that all of France knows what he means.

"To buy some bullets, also," Wa says, knowing he hasn't said it well. He adds, "My gun, that gun, here." He moves the paper to the side and taps the glass with a finger.

"Not yet, it's not."

It's easy. "*Arrête tes conneries, toi.*"

"What?"

"*Rien.* Noth."

"*What?*"

"Cont. *Cont.*"

"*What?*"

The guy walks away watching him while Wa gives him Bruce Willis's smallsmile. He knows there are other gunshops and wants to tell this *mec* exactly that, but he's afraid if he goes to another gunshop he'll have new weeks to wait. He hopes the guy doesn't come back to him with questions, more test questions. Even to the question, "Why do you want this gun?" he won't know what to say that would pass. There are lots of answers. One is, Because then I have a gun to show you outside the store. He remembers, yes, *egalité* is an answer. *Egalité*: a gun in America is the big equalizer, is what little Devito said once, pointing a gun at a huge unbelievable asshole.

The *mec* reappears from the backroom with the guy Wa likes. "Him," he hears the *mec* say. Both look Wa over. They don't know he can hear them.

"We gotta do a psych on this one."

"Too late."

"He's gonna go postal, man," the *mec* says, and Wa understands that they have the same expression here. In France it's *à la postal*, only there they use acid for the face, probably because of no gunshops. Wa shrugs at them from a distance like a helpful friend.

"He ain't gonna go postal."

"*Look* at the guy."

"Paperwork's through."

"*I'm* not selling it to him."

The guy he likes shakes his head, says fuck, and comes on over.

"How you wanna pay," he asks, picking up and eyeing the paper, "Roy?"

"*Plastique.*" Wa snaps his mother's Visa card flat to the glass. "The bullets, also."

"*Yes*, one puts beanbag chair into taxi," Wa grunts at the driver, shoving. He knows it's true because this is the second time he's had to. This time, his mother has turfed him, so he's moving.

"*Yes* beanbag *puts* in *Americain* taxi," Wa insists, getting his shoulder into it.

The driver comes out and around and helps with his cowboy boot. Wa loves his chair. It's brown, thick and Spanish and expensive and very heavy. The lady said it's bullfight-killed leather and showed him the sword hole with tape over it to keep the beans in. Wa wants to joke with the driver, Where are Algerians when you need? The driver gives the chair an extra last kick with his heel and gets the door closed. Wa gets in front with the driver, wincing when he sits. The gun has moved in the struggle with the chair and is badly poking his spine, which is of course a huge vein with a bone around it.

"Where to?" The driver has put on a ball cap instead of pulling the windshield visor down, which Wa sees is broken. The sun is badly eye to eye this evening and Wa has to squint. He thinks that in it he can see the weird green from all the corn out there. He has come to learn that his home state exists to grow food for pigs, but he still likes his chosen city. On the driver's cap is a cartoon wild Indian, mouth wide open in a baseball cheer.

"I move," Wa says.

The driver steps softly on the brake and the car slows. He doesn't look at Wa this time when he asks him the same question.

"To here." Wa passes him the paper he pulls from his pocket.

Reading Wa's mother's writing, the driver mumbles, "Home-Lite Men's Shelter," nods, then touches the brake again and tells Wa he wants to see some money first.

Wa hates the *mec* now and breathes *cont* as he gathers all the coins from his coat pockets. It would be easy to skilfully undo the driver's shirt buttons with his gun. He could knock out one molar. But he feels like *un bébé* with these coins like this, cupped in both hands. Last night he tried to count it, but he is not used to the small *monnaie* here.

"Just the quarters," the driver says, and drives.

Wa didn't really think his mother would turf him, but she did. He had no idea he had maxed her *plastique*. In Paris her *plastique* was immortal. The gun was some hundreds, the chair was some hundreds, then it was only food and DVD rent. But last night she pointed and screamed, "Look at you — it's not like *I'm* spending money on food," which was true because she was going skinny again. She didn't believe him that he had tried to get jobs a few times, walking into stores and going up to the guy or babe behind the counter and asking, "Job?" and waiting for what happened next. Usually nothing did, but one babe did go get a smiling boss, only then it all sort of fell apart with the test questions, and Wa's answers that didn't pass.

Des Moines has become uglier, a part of town Wa doesn't know. It makes him think of two words he's learned, "mullet" and "scree." He understands he's going down the rungs of success, not up, and that he's not going to get his hot tub anytime soon, which is a huge, huge drag. But he will get his neck brace

— tomorrow he has the doctor's appointment his mother arranged for him. Wa was surprised to see that you can't just buy them. But he will get one and it will be excellent. Maybe it alone will complete his dream. He sees himself sitting wonderfully in the men's shelter, in his beanbag chair, cleaning his gun, watching the DVD *Tarte d'Amerique Numero Trois*, or any movie, *ce n'est pas important*. Not important what movie because he is wearing his neck brace. Not important if he gets bored with his gun because he is wearing his neck brace. Wearing his neck brace, he has only to tilt his head but several millimetres and fall so comfortably to sleep. Why do so few Americans wear neck braces?

Here in the taxi, unbraced, Wa's head pivots to see even more fast food places in this part of Des Moines. He knows the real reason his mother turfed him. It's not because he drained her *plastique*, it's because he is shaping like a pear. He looks enough like her in the face that it scares her to death to look at him and see this shape of her nightmares. He tried joking — *J'arrive! Ta poire!* — displaying himself with arms up and doing a big round hula, but it failed to stop her horror. Sometimes he caught her staring across the room at the dent — the big dent plus the little gun-dent — his new pear ass had made in the beanbag chair.

Yes, everybody in America is mad at Wa.

"Where put?" Wa points to one corner of the huge room of beds, then to another corner. There is no DVD, or even TV set, to point to. It must be in another huge room.

"Listen to me: *No private furniture in common areas.*"

The man is right, there *is* no furniture, which is a perfect reason for Wa to place his chair somewhere. The man is not much older than Wa but bald, and his head shiny with what looks like a coating of aspic. And he is angry. Before him, the taxi driver was angry when Wa spilled so many nickels and pennies onto the seat. Before that, Wa's mother.

"Where put?" Wa points again, this time at a staircase which might lead somewhere, maybe to a special bedroom for Wa.

"*It stays outside.*" The man begins to roll the beanbag chair across the floor, past the counter with the thick glass, toward the door Wa had rolled it in. Behind the thick glass, sitting on a desk, is a small TV for the bald man alone. On the TV is Iraq, but not in colour. Sometimes Iraq seemed not in colour even on his mother's TV, because the soldiers and tanks and sand and buildings were all so excellently coordinated in beige.

"Out?"

"*Out.*"

Wa stops the chair by stamping his foot in front of it.

"Bullfight kill!" He points to the tape covering the sword hole. If the man knows how great this chair is, it will get a place of importance. The man might want it for himself, but this is the chance Wa takes.

"What?"

"Bullfight kill." Wa points, stabbing, at the tape. He remembers the lady called it duck tape. "Under duck, *là*."

"*What?*"

Wa pulls his gun from the back of his pants, points it at the tape, makes shooting noises, and explains, "Kill! Kill!"

But the bald man doesn't understand.

Wa has been in the alley some hours now. From the pink and orange clouds above his head it looks like the sun is lying down. He wants to find another alley because another *clochard* is using his chair. This one he can smell from some feet away. Wa will have to wash his chair when the *clochard* moves.

There are no bullets in Wa's gun (his mother is on the pills again and last week when Wa's pizza *mec* knocked on the door she screamed and flushed all sorts of stuff — pills, powders, Wa's bullets — down the toilet) but the bald Home-Lite man said he was calling the police, so Wa rolled the chair out the door on his own. He wondered why all this excitement over a gun in America. He rolled his heavy chair down the street, then up an alley, where he found a place for it behind a bright yellow Dumpster. He was very tired and felt very fat but didn't want to breathe this hard because he was sucking in the smell here. It was difficult to find a spot for the chair that wasn't wet with something. Wa saw a police car zip past the mouth of the alley, then again, the same car. He sat on his chair and soon fell asleep with his head back against the brick wall, not a bad neck brace except in only one direction.

The first *clochard* woke him with a soft kick to the leg. He asked if Wa had anything to drink. The man was dark and at first Wa thought he was a towel-head, but then he saw that he was just dirty, and also very pale, the colour of *champignons*. Another man came, then another, and a black one, and one who Wa was certain was a red Indian, and some of them came with something to drink — Wa tried a tiny sip, which burned his throat and then made him want to puke — and he learned that these men came here each evening to wait for the Home-Lite Shelter to open its door. They asked one another, many times, what they thought the soup and sandwich would be, and Wa understood that the menu changed every night.

But it is three dirty men who have now taken and used his chair. It is *communistique*. When Paris had a *communiste* mayor Wa's mother wanted to move to Luxembourg. She hates communists more than anything — though she would hate these American *clochard* communists less because none of them are fat. They are exactly not fat — their thinness is almost like hers. (Though his mother is confused, lately, about fat Americans. At first she smiled and said, "They make me feel so thin and they are everywhere." And then, staring with eyes of hate at Wa himself, she said, "They are disgusting and there are more of them every day.") She once told Wa that communists are exactly why she's not rich, and that once they sprayed chicken blood on her furs during a show, and trying to kick one in the face from her catwalk she ruined her ankle for *la saison*. Here in this alley, this particular communist stinks and won't get out of Wa's chair.

"Please, up?" Wa asks the communist thief, nudging the man's foot with his own.

"You one funny dude, know tha'?" a black *clochard* tells him again. The *nigre* smiles and smiles and has him by the inner elbow and is squeezing. His teeth aren't as white as in the movies and neither are his eyes, they are full of *café au lait*, and one eye aims itself the wrong way, off into nothing.

Wa goes to piss where the others go to piss, ten steps away. When he returns he sees that the sleeping *clochard* American communist has puked. None has hit the leather, but the thin pool on the cement is trying to find a direction and it looks like it wants to go to the chair. Once at a wild zoo near Versailles, Wa was near a turkey when it shit and this pool of vomit smells *exactement comme la même*.

"Up!" Wa pokes the communist in the forehead with his sudden gun.

All around him the communists yell *Jesus shit* and *holy cow* and *easy*. The sick communist's eyes finally open, then open wide, and now his hands are in the sky like a western.

"*Allez!*"

The *clochard* rolls off the chair and crawls away on his hands and knees. Wa looks and sees that the alley is now empty.

He shoves his gun down the front of his pants — with no bullets, veins are *pas important* — and rolls the chair away from the puke. He keeps rolling it, down the alley to another alley, because the communists might be phoning the police. He rolls it past the back door of a small *boîte* with country music banging out, past a dry cleaners with its breath of poison, past brick wall after brick wall, and finally past the steamed windows and wonderful smell of a bakery, where he stops, inhaling deeply.

Catching his breath, Wa imagines the soup and sandwiches he could have had at the shelter, pictures the communists stuffing their greedy faces with free food, laughing about the fool Wa who has nothing. The thing with America is, when you eat a lot of burgers, you begin to need a lot of burgers. It has been two days since Wa has had a burger, or anything at all. He sits in his chair to think. He is instantly comfortable, it is an excellent chair. He truly does not wish to sell it, though all day that thought has been hiding in the trees of his brain like the limping monster in a black-and-white. He shifts his ass at the discomfort of this idea and he hears the rattle of beans. No, his stomach hears the beans, and a funny idea comes — he is sitting on a *vachement* bag of food. Even the bag is food — if you soaked and cooked his chair you would have a *cassoulet* for one hundred people!

Amidst Wa's sad chuckles he suffers another vision of the free sandwiches. Then recalls, in a glorious burst of hope, another place: the restaurants across the street from each other, their signs shouting free fries. Wa almost faints.

It has taken him maybe three hours to find the street. He rolled his chair kilometres, mostly in alleys, before finding enough cardboard, and several branches from sidewalk trees, to cover and hide it. Wa is exhausted, but feels even more sorry for the chair, which is white around the side from being scraped on so much pavement.

Wa is more than hungry when he rounds the corner and there they are — the two restaurants. He goes to them as fast as he can. He is limping now, he is the monster coming out of the trees. Perhaps some water will be free too. And ketchup. And *vinegre*. And salt, and pepper, and of course the glorious fat the perfect potatoes are cooked in. Wa almost faints again.

He is under the sign of the first restaurant. There is the "free" and the "fries." Wa pushes the door and his wrists buckle when it doesn't open. Wa sees the darkness inside, the *café* is closed. He is already turning away, one hand out in the direction of the other café, when he registers his face in the glass door — his is the dark face of not only a towel-head, but also the dirty face of a *clochard* communist thief.

Wa stumbles across the street to the music of three honking horns. He is smiling because he has read on the other sign not just the "free" and the "fries," but also the words "all" and "nite." And its windows glow like an inn for hobbits.

The door opens to his push. Inside, in chairs, sit Americans of all shapes — round, pear, or bony. It is not a rich place, and some are nearly *clochards*. Wa walks as near as he can to the smell of food itself, to a long counter with stools. Wa chooses the stool in the middle of no people. He knows that now he, too, smells. How huge his smell he does not know, but he knows he never smelled this way in Paris. It has been a major surprise: in America, you must work so hard.

The waitress comes smiling with a pad and pen, her eyebrows up. She is plump and knows nothing of fashion. Wa finds her beautiful because she is unlike his mother in every way. She is beautiful because she will bring him food.

"Fry." *Non.* "Fry–zzz." In *Americain*, Wa always forgets the *s* sound. He flaps his hand in the direction of the sign outside, to make sure she understands.

"Large? Small?"

"Big," says Wa, surprised that he is allowed a choice. He gives her a joke with an eager smile: "Very, *very*, big!"

"And what else?" the waitress asks. "Anything?"

Wa doesn't know what to say. The waitress helps him.

"Some gravy with the fries?"

"Yes!"

"Anything else?"

"Water?"

"Certainly."

"Ketchup?" Wa lifts the ketchup bottle beside the salt and pepper. He raises his eyebrows in question.

The waitress spins away laughing. To her back he asks "*Vinegre?*" but feels greedy for it.

Because he can smell the kitchen, waiting is magical. Because he sits in front of the window ledge onto which the chefs place hot platters of food, the waiting is Fellini. He sees burgers, he sees a *steak frites,* he sees pastas with red sauce and with white. Baskets of garlic toast, an omelette heaped with *champignons.* Finally, in front of him, clunked down by the beautiful waitress, his fries, the large plate centred by a *demi-tasse* of gravy, thick *jus.* All of it steams under Wa's head, the heat and smell releasing the flesh of his face. Wa groans, eats.

And he finishes. He cannot really remember eating it, but he knows that what just happened was *superb*. The waitress has refilled his water twice. Wa has licked the gravy glass clean. Not a speck of potato remains. He sits on his stool, head in one hand, sighing, wishing he had some food remaining in his mouth, to suck and fondle with his tongue.

But Wa rises, catches the waitress's eye, calls "tankyouvelly-much," and makes to leave.

"Sir? You have to pay?" The waitress waves a small yellow paper at him. She is smiling.

"No!"Wa smiles too. He points a finger in the direction of the sign outside. "*Gratis?* Fry flee. Flies. *Fries.*"

"Beg pardon, sir?"

"Fries."

"That's right. You have to pay for them."

Wa shakes his head, smiling instructively, pointing at the sign. "Mais, non!"

The waitress turns her head, says, "Tommy." A big chef comes out. He stands at her side and she whispers to him. Both of them watch Wa. Wa, trying to look friendly, shrugs for them. He is tired, he is *vachement fatigué*. He hears mumbles from either side of him. Someone shouts, "Pay the lady." He thinks he hears the word "towel-head." A few chairs scrape on the floor, two or three people stand. One man is fat, but fat like the Hells Angels always called Tiny.

The chef asks him, "You got a problem?"

Yes. He is very tired. He might not be able to find his bean-bag chair in the dark, this chair that he would now sell, would gladly give them to pay for his fries. They have lied to him, things are not free in America. He wants to cry like a *bébé*. He wants to go pound on his mother's door. He thinks his pear-shape is almost gone from today's work alone and maybe she will let him in. She will say, *Arrête tes conneries toi*, and hug him.

He thinks of words he needs. Trade? Swap?

"Swat," he tells the chef and the waitress.

"What?"

"Tray."

"*What?*"

Wa pulls his gun from the front of his pants. It is worth one hundred or one million plates of *frites* and they can have it and he only wants to go. He hardly gets the gun up to show its huge value when one side of the room explodes and hits him. The other side of the room explodes too, he is knocked two ways. Now he is on the floor staring at the ceiling and he is deaf. At his stomach he puts his hand to a fire, here, and here, and when he sees his hand it is so red with the greasiest blood. The room is full of smoke that stinks and chokes — he had no clue how gunshots would take over a room and conquer everything like this.

Faces appear above him. He sees mouths working hard but most just stare. The fiery pain is somewhere distant. He is deaf but it is at the same time a roaring. He feels the deep-hose and the draining — it is a surprise but *exactement* the kind he knew it would be. He works his mouth like a fish that's alive and being cleaned in the rudest kitchen. Some faces drop closer. Maybe he should tell them he is *American*, in case they've not understood, but there's no easy way to say this. He could tell them, "Roy," but that is not his name. He wants to say, "*Roi*," but his tongue won't roll. It has drained.

"Wa," he says. He has nothing to tell them that's important.

A WORK-IN-PROGRESS

A nthony Ott was in town tonight, said the poster. He would be reading from his latest work.

Theo studied the somewhat famous face. Stark black and white, the photocopy shouted Ott's hollows and crags. His eyes were inscrutable blots. It was more a Rorschach than a face.

Theo caught himself memorizing the address. Why in heaven's hell would he want to hear Ott again? That time twenty years ago had been so horrible. He thought about it still. The spectacle. Ott singling him out, shouting, emphasizing the "you."

Since then, Theo hadn't bought any of Ott's books. In bookstores he found himself avoiding looking at their covers. Eight o'clock, Theo whispered, scanning the poster.

Also he hated readings on principle. He never went to one voluntarily. In the four years at this university he had often been forced by committee — risk to tenure was never mentioned, but there it was — to take on the chore of hosting yet another minor writer. A campus tour, dinner, then the reading itself, Theo sitting with ten or so self-conscious others in a sterile room of empty chairs, wishing he had a bottle of wine, a magazine, or — blasphemy, given what he did for a living — a mini-TV so he could watch the ball game.

Even that first reading, long ago, had been reluctant. It was a date, a first date, with fellow grad student Oona. A prof had mentioned a reading by some new writer named Ott and, later that night, there they were, driving to the suburban library, neither Theo nor Oona wanting to be the one to venture that this idea sounded a little dry. They'd been coolly discussing how the word *carnal* formed the hot root of the *carnivalesque,* and both wanted nothing more than to find a bed somewhere, which they did eventually do, and did again and again for years until their sole reason for being together rubbed itself out.

Eight o'clock. A converted church. Theo stood before looming wooden doors, posters of Ott's face taped to them. He'd actually done it. He'd come, once more, to hear Anthony Ott read.

People filed by as he stood at the threshold. He had not yet committed himself. He would ponder this a moment. Why had he come? Was he bored? No. Did he want to relive memories of Oona? No. Youth? No. He was proudly pragmatic. He never loved what wasn't there.

So why? He felt a yawning in the gut. Ott had shouted, See *you* again.

Not that Ott could pull what he pulled last time, not with this many people — ten had pushed past him into the church in the last minute alone. The other time there had been just him, Oona and two old ladies. And Ott. In a windowless back room of the Valley Library, Ott had loomed over them there in the front row. The only row. Maybe that had been part of Ott's problem, that so few had come to hear him read.

Bearded, dark, he'd had an Abraham Lincoln severity, without the height. His eyes were wise, but also mean. In an academic hierarchy logical to Theo at the time, Ott's wisdom gave him the right to be mean. He'd looked at the four of them in turn, then shaken his head and, well, sneered. At the scant number perhaps, or at what he'd seen, or not seen, in their eyes. It had made Theo nervous and, for some reason, ashamed.

Ott read from what he called a work-in-progress. It sounded like poetry. Odd syntax, obscure allusion, images that when given close enough attention granted a rustle in some dusk-lit thicket of the brain. Actually, Theo didn't listen much. Oona's bare knee was against his. Theo answered her pressure. She increased hers. He his. At one point, with Ott ten minutes into it, Theo's and Oona's legs were shaking in a push-of-war, and they were trying hard not to laugh.

Ott eventually finished, informed them that the book he had just read from was to be called *The Lobe*, then looked Theo in the eye and asked, loud, "Why did you come?"

"Me?" Theo asked. He couldn't tell if Ott had seen their game-playing, or if the question was simply interest.

"Why did you come?" Ott asked again. His expression wouldn't change.

"Ah, I wanted to hear you read. We" — best get Oona in on this, take some of the heat — "wanted to hear you read."

"I'm nobody. Do you go to every reading in town?"

"No." Theo almost added "sir."

"Tell me why you came. Tell me the truth."

Ott leaned onto his podium and he hung out over Theo, barely three feet away. Theo felt his face go red. He shrugged.

"I don't know." He turned to Oona and tried a joke. "Hey, why did we come here? I thought we were going to *Rocky II*."

"How long," Ott asked, "have you wanted to be a writer?"

"What?" Why torture just him? There were three others here.

"You want to be a writer, don't you?"

"No. I dunno. Maybe. I've thought about it."

"So tell me a story."

Theo laughed weakly. He looked over at Oona, and she grimaced in sympathy. He tossed back at Ott, "I'll write one and mail it to you."

"Come on." Anthony Ott's stare was now severe. "Tell me a story."

"I can't just —"

"*Fucking tell me a story.*"

One old lady gasped. Theo glanced over. She gathered up her sweater, to leave. The other old lady was smiling.

Ott loomed over him, relentless. What the hell. A story. "Once upon a time, there was a boy and a girl with nothing to do. What they really wanted to do was go play doctor. Instead they went and hear a big man read a storybook." Theo wasn't saying this out loud, of course. "The big man read his storybook a long long time and put everyone to sleep . . ." Some bizarre part of his brain was telling this to the main part that was shy and outraged. Here he was a minute away from sex with Oona in his parked car, and this monstrous bohemian was humiliating him.

"When the story was over," Theo said to himself, watching Oona sort of smiling at Ott, "the man got very bossy and the boy began to cry —"

"No story to tell?" asked Ott. He was smiling sarcastically, packing his briefcase.

"— and he decided never, ever to buy that man's books."

Ott was leaving. Speak up now or forever hold . . .

At the door Ott turned and waved to the empty room, wearing a cheery smile. He pointed at Theo and said, "See *you* again."

Theo stood at the church doors, still undecided, when a nondescript fellow, the host, likely a lit drone clinging to tenure like himself, came out and, though there was no reason to whisper, whispered, "We're starting."

Theo looked for a seat. The place was packed. Sixty or so people had come to listen to Anthony Ott. A single empty seat in the front row, in front of the podium. Anyone sitting in the front row would be Ott fans. Would people think that of him too if he took that seat, even if it was the only seat?

Theo made his way to the glaring chair. He made a show of scanning back over the room, and shrugging before he sat down. And then he pointedly looked at his watch.

Suddenly Ott entered from the side. He strode to the podium, dishevelled, preoccupied, utterly not nervous, as though this reading were just another of the day's chores.

Theo stared up at the man. Twenty years. There was something obvious and repulsive about the bastard still.

Ott snapped open a battered briefcase and lifted out a stack of paper that he thunked onto a shelf inside the podium. Age hadn't changed Anthony Ott much. A few pounds, some grey hair. Mostly, he looked twenty years wiser and meaner.

"I'll read from a work-in-progress," he announced, looking down, shuffling the unseen stack. Theo hated it when he couldn't see the paper. He liked watching a pile dwindle, liked being able to tell how much longer the ordeal would go on.

Ott looked up suddenly, as if remembering where he was.

He began searching the eyes of the audience. He didn't hurry. Seat by seat, he met eyes. People began to shuffle. It was dreadful. Theo heard a snicker. Ott continued his scan. When he was almost through, almost up to Theo himself, Ott threw a match into the fumes of unease by saying, "I wonder why you're here."

The hall went into high fidget.

A vague dread had been growing in Theo's stomach ever since he first sat down. When their eyes did meet, Theo knew. In relation to Ott, he was sitting in the same spot exactly as on that horrid night past. Theo jolted upright with *déjà vu*. His spine rang. They started at each other. It was like decades had passed in a night's sleep.

Ott's eyes moved on. But his lids had lifted in recognition, Theo was sure of it.

"Anyone with ideas for a title for this thing of mine," Ott announced, a sneer prying up his lip, "I'll gladly consider it." Some people laughed. "Not good at titles," he added. More laughs, though Ott had sounded serious.

Ott began to read. Theo did try to listen. Readings were torture.

It went like this: Ott described someone named Marty, a man who saw people as "scared carcasses fleeing a death so inevitable it had somehow already happened." Theo got caught pondering this notion and missed the next bit, about Marty reliving his mother's breast whenever he smelled a certain fabric. Or when he *felt* a certain fabric? Angry to have missed it, he missed some more. Now Ott was onto someone named Lulu. Lulu was a girlfriend, a woman obsessed with birds ever since she heard they'd evolved from dinosaurs.

". . . her mind cradled the freshly ancient miracle," Ott read, looking up, "of a brontosaurus taking wing in the body of a tweeting finch . . ."

Theo half-heard all this. He was trying to recall Ott titles, none of which he'd read. *The Chrome Harpsichord*? *Call Me 46*? Weren't those two?

Theo sat up with a jerk. Ott was staring hard at him, saying, ". . . the worst part was that in public places Marty loved to point out any big or little step and say to her, 'Watch out. It's a lulu.'"

It was a big-eyed, accusing look. The bastard. The arrogance. What right had he to single out a daydreamer and stare at him? This wasn't school.

". . . her comeback with a louder 'Real funny, Marty' always saw him instantly defeated, and recalculating the arithmetic of their love . . ."

Had Ott indeed recognized him? He was back reading from the page now. Or was he just pretending to read? His lips moved, but not his eyes.

What had happened that night? Theo had left the library with an ugly, unfinished feeling. Motives shrouded, meanings hanging. He'd told Ott he wanted to be a writer. It was the only time he told anybody that. He hadn't even been sure of it himself until he heard himself say it out loud.

Theo had not become a writer. But neither was he jealous of writers, though Oona had accused him of this that night as he punched his bed between fits of lovemaking, cursing Ott. Oona assured him over and over that Ott hadn't made a fool of him, that Theo had stood his ground. Yet all through their relationship, whenever Theo tore into any writer, living or dead (which was his job as a student of literature, after all), Oona would say to him, simply, like it was truth, "You're jealous."

He'd given it a try. But it was almost as though he was too smart for creativity. It was like he knew too much in advance, his brain a wary seer that predicted a mistake before it was even made. Theo saw this but could not stop it. Every good idea was analyzed to woodenness before it was typed down and, after several years of such trying, he quit. But he was not jealous. He'd admitted to himself without terror that the part of him that in childhood had been able to "make stuff up" was hidden from him, or lost. It was not a big deal. Intellect had overcome a certain instinct, a certain spontaneity. That was all. He was not jealous.

Eyes. Theo remembered where he was. Ott was staring at him again.

". . . and the scabrous fur falling in handfuls from Marty's dog Mica drove Lulu nearly wild . . ."

When Theo met his eye, Ott turned back to his pages. But it did indeed seem he was not reading at all. Theo hadn't heard the crisply onomatopoetic *flip* of a page in some time now. Ott was merely talking. Or had he memorized his stuff? Was that possible?

". . . it was birds she wanted. Birds. Birds! Flight. A pet at home in space. Not the mud blood bone tongue of dogs . . ."

Theo checked his watch. Ott had been reading now for almost a half hour. A decent reading lasted forty minutes. An excellent reading lasted thirty.

Theo hoped Ott would at least be decent. He waited for voice intonations to rise to a final peaking sentence. He recalled one poet he'd hosted who had read on and on, almost an hour and a half. It was always lesser writers who read longest. Once they lucked onto a stage they refused to let it go. Toward the end, over shuffling feet, the poet had read faster and faster, his face pale. Another thing about readings, Theo decided now, was that writers deserved whatever they got.

". . . on his sixteenth birthday Marty received from his folks a truckload of dirt dumped in the back yard. He was invited to level it and plant the vegetation of his choice . . ."

So Ott had memorized this stuff. He was definitely no longer reading. He stared at the ceiling, or over the heads of the audience. And at Theo.

". . . as far as the more exotic plants went, all he got was a single cantaloupe the size and shape of a cat's head, those sleekly flattened and sinister planes . . ."

On and on and on. The reading approached the hour mark. The next time Ott eyed him, he would look pointedly at his watch.

". . . it was Lulu's magic with flowers that seduced him. She could entice from dirt blooms the likes of which no one thereabouts had seen, blooms so huge with colour they shrieked, were almost frightening . . ."

On and on. Perhaps Theo slept. Because, when it came, the shout from several rows back had the effect of jolting him awake.

"Not this time, Ott!" a man yelled. A chair scudded on the floor.

Theo turned with everyone else to see a young fellow with wild hair stumbling out of his row. He wasn't looking at Ott. He made it to the aisle and stomped out of the church, mumbling.

Ott watched the retreating man. His voice rose as if following him out the door.

"Well. Suddenly, one day Marty just stopped growing things. He just gave up. Woe to him. Big mistake."

Ott looked down again to his pages, though Theo was certain now he wasn't reading.

". . . his new hobby was no more than a distraction for his failure at flowers . . ."

"You win!" someone yelled just behind Theo's head, making him jump. "That's enough! You win!"

Theo turned. A hefty man behind him stood, red-faced, pointing at Ott. He held a suitcase. The airplane tags dangling from the handle looked fresh.

"I'm out of it!" the hefty man yelled. He shoved his way out of his row and clomped puffing out of the church.

Ott read calmly on. A tiny smile lifted the corners of his mouth.

". . . distractions, one after another, blocking all light from a life. The travel, the TV and brownies and cookies and more of Auntie Em's chili and cornbread and, my goodness, Marty spun like a top in his search for the next wee thing to fill his skinny time . . ."

Theo wondered hard about leaving. He heard others get up, some quietly, some with a grumble. He heard whispers of grievance, of attempted mutiny. He thought he could hear one man softly weeping.

Theo didn't want to leave. He realized he was enjoying himself for the first time since it had started, over an hour ago. He looked at his watch. An hour and a half ago. Which was enough, he joked to himself, to make any man cry.

He sat back in his chair. Perhaps Ott had a kind of cult following, people who travelled to all his readings, like fans of the Grateful Dead. Theo swivelled and checked out the audience. About a third had gone. The remainder looked to be of two types. One group seemed confused. They sat politely but wanted to leave. This strange author had gone on far too long, they seemed to be thinking. The other group was more resolute, angry, used to it. They looked dug in.

". . . there's a twist to this tale, that will without fail, save us from ruin, as sure as the mail . . ."

God, the maniac was rhyming now. Theo listened. He heard iambic and dactylic, enjambment and inversion. Marty and Lulu kept popping in and out, as if to keep up the pretense of a story. But it all made a sort of sense, Theo thought, it seemed to be about something almost vital. Almost, well, personal. One's dirty underwear, or something. Theo could not put his finger on it. Whenever he thought he had, he realized he'd missed the next bit, the next clue, and his logic fell apart.

". . . Marty went to bed. Marty slept all night long. Marty got up. Marty washed. Marty looked out the window. He said, Hello Mr. Sun. He had a good breakfast. Good Marty. Where was Lulu? Good Lulu. Lulu was not there. Lulu was not with Marty . . ."

This was some kind of challenge, Theo decided. The church was now a quarter full. A dozen people. One man was snoring loudly, but it sounded fake, a provocation. Ott kept going, looking perfectly at ease. Twenty minutes later the snorer left.

". . . Lulu sat in her kitchen too. Picture a split picture. He and her, staring at their phones. Lulu's phone is off the hook. She knows that Marty knows it's off the hook. And she knows that Marty knows that she knows that he knows. And she knows that Marty knows that she knows that Marty knows that she . . ."

Theo looked up. He had decided. He no longer considered Ott a profoundly irritating human but rather a kind of natural force. An unclimbed mountain whose obstacles were boredom and spite. Ott walking in and opening his mouth had been a challenge from the start. An arrogant dare, a slap in the face with verbosity's gaudy white glove.

Theo would meet Ott's challenge. Whatever the game, Theo was going to win.

By midnight, four hours since the start, only Theo and one other man were left. Theo turned his seat around to study him. He was young, thirtyish, dressed in a blue track suit. He looked in shape. He looked prepared. He sat erect, eyes closed. He was either asleep or in the bosom of some Eastern discipline.

Theo listened and didn't listen. Ott was now into Marty's childhood.

"... with a pure innocence, Marty squished the frog. He was as innocent as the frog itself whenever it long-tongued a bug. Now it was frog's turn to be a bug, Marty's to be frog. Sacred teeter and totter. Profane reason had not yet intruded on Marty ..."

Theo drifted in and out. Sometimes he sought daydreams so as to escape Ott's words, some of which nonetheless slipped in and poked him. He tried to recall Oona but couldn't, not her face. Parts of her body, yes. Which perhaps summed up their time together. He could recall the feeling of being inside her, as distinct from being inside other women. He could recall her voice too, he'd loved her voice. They'd had some good times. Lying in bed, no hurry, savage in their desire, no plan to life. How long you could sustain that kind of life was of course the whole —

"Marty oh Marty oh Marty!" Ott shrieked, imitating Lulu's voice. It sounded like Olive Oyl in *Popeye*. "How could you how could you how could you ...?"

Theo thought of problems at work. Funding cuts for low enrolment courses. A tedious faculty in general, older types who talked Chaucer and Pope even in the lounge. Lately Theo had been admitting to himself that he didn't much like his job. To admit that about his life's work was, well, horrible. But how many people truly liked their work? In their heart of hearts how many? The word itself was tiring. *Work* was synonymous with struggle. *Struggle* was onomatopoeia for *work*. *Work* was anathema to *play*. By definition work should not be liked.

One-thirty. Oooh, he'd be tired tomorrow. He had to prep a lecture. Virginia Woolf. Stream of . . . Jesus, he should just bring the class here, this loon would probably still be at it. Ott looked depressingly fresh.

". . . No, I said, 'Lulu, will you MARRY me?' That's what I said. I didn't say, 'Lulu, you scare me.' Why the hell would I say that? Because I do I do I do want to marry you . . ."

At a quarter to three Theo jolted upright at a crash behind him. The fellow in the track suit had toppled, chair and all. He lay on the floor and didn't move. Perhaps he was dead.

Theo announced in wonder, "Just *me* now," somewhat helplessly stating the obvious.

"Please don't interrupt," Ott hissed at him, glaring before turning back to his paper. "So Marty decided to read a book. What to read was always a problem because his library was so vast, taking up four walls in one room, and six walls in another . . ."

"Come on!" Theo yelled, out of anger and fear both. "What the hell! Let's go home!"

"Be quiet or I'll ask you to leave . . . Books stacked on the toilet back, up to the ceiling. Books filling the cellar, inured to the cold floor. Last time he was down there he'd plucked an obscure Tolstoy from the mouse dust and shouted *Da!* like an overt Russian and curled up with it, on the spot, for two days and nights . . ."

Theo flopped back into his seat. He was sweating. It was the middle of the night. Rain pattered on the roof of the church.

His dog would be whimpering in his spot under the eaves. His class tomorrow would be a disaster.

Theo stared at Ott. The writer was clinging to his lectern for support. He was holding his chin up, fighting gravity. He was definitely tiring.

". . . the King of Persia had amnesia," Ott trilled in a raspy attempt at a little girl's voice. ". . . and tried to rob the store. Apackalips, apocalypse, he went back again for more . . ."

The lunatic was rhyming again. Theo stood up. He waggled a finger, groping for words.

"You just made that up. It doesn't count."

Ott stopped and looked up at Theo. His brows rose in supercilious innocence.

"This is my novel-in-progress. Please don't interrupt."

"A novel? You're saying this is a novel? Okay, where does that Persia thing fit in? And what does it mean?"

"It was Lulu's rhyme. She is a child and she's skipping. You think a child's rhyme must . . ." Ott pronounced the next word as if it crawled with maggots ". . . 'mean'? You an English professor?"

Theo said nothing.

"Be quiet or I will be forced to stop." Ott paused like a shark before the fatal bite. "Would you . . . like me to stop?"

Two very distinct sides of Theo's mind had a quick, shocking fight, and the perverse side won.

"Of course not." Theo had his own sense of timing. "I came all this way."

He watched Ott for a sign of disappointment or fear, but saw nothing. Ott merely continued. He wore the tiniest smile.

"Lulu wound her skip-rope in a tight figure eight and went in for lunch. For fuel. For the past ten minutes her nostrils had been wide and ripe in anticipation of her daily Velveeta . . ."

Oh, but Theo was hungry. Ott must be too. Expending all that energy. Look at him, still bobbing his head for emphasis, still gazing out at a crowd that wasn't there. The rain had stopped. His voice rang louder in the silence.

Oh, my. Crazy, crazy. Ott, Ott, wouldn't stop, wouldn't stop and wouldn't drop, talking till his head went pop. There, put that in your "novel." I can do drivel too, Mr. Writer. Why am I listening to you, not you to me? Old old Anthony Ott, drops his trousers on the spot. Behind the dais lurks a penis. Against the podium he bumps his scrotium.

Why the hell had he given up on writing, anyway? Maybe he should try again, quite the analytical maze. Right, quit his job at his age. He was thinking crazy. Oh, it was late.

"Would you like to go for coffee?"

Ott had spoken to him. He had stopped reading and asked a question. He had distinctly said, Would you like to go for a coffee. Theo sprang to his feet and punched his fist in the air.

"Yes! Coffee!" he shouted. "I win! Me! I win!"

Theo stood teetering. He grinned, puffing. Ott was watching him. A smile rose like sewer water.

"Please shut up," Ott said calmly, smile peaking in a sneer. "Don't interrupt. MARTIN has just asked LULU if she cared to join him for coffee. It's pivotal."

Theo stood breathing through his mouth. He stared past Ott into the velvet-curtained gloom of the empty stage. Ott cleared his throat and continued.

". . . 'Java preference where we go?' Martin asked of his love. 'It shouldn't mocha lot of difference . . .'"

Theo quietly took his chair. It was getting light out. The door opened and he turned to see a janitor enter, take a fearful look at them, and begin sweeping. Ott's voice gained volume.

"...Marty suggested that in their role as custodians of truth, the lumpen should never jumpen to conclusions..."

Theo couldn't quit, couldn't let the bastard win. Ott looked too content, in a bliss of his own making. Somehow he knew he had in his grip a professor of literature.

During Ott's pauses, Theo could hear birds out on the eaves. Beaky gibberish. Parliament of fowls. Nature mocking him too.

Such noise. Theo opened his eyes to darkness. He could hardly breathe. Where in hell was he. His spine arched in pain.

Awareness limped in. Theo discovered that his face lay on his knees, his nose pinched between them. His arms hung down, knuckles scraping gritty linoleum. The noise was a dreadful monotone voice. Theo remembered where he was.

"... Phenomenology is a body of heavily thought thoughts aimed at that beyond thought. While we work hard thinking, Phenomeness dances with her girly grin, singing Nya nya nya nya nyaaa nya. We can hear her tune, some nights, issuing from the stars ..."

Anger fuelled a burst of adrenalin. Trailing a wire of saliva, Theo's head lifted off his knees.

"Bullshit!" Theo croaked. "You're babbling!"

"... that's what Phenomeness sings, SAID LULU, AS MARTY WOKE FROM HIS NAP."

"That's a trick. Doesn't count. You're just making it up."

Ott sneered joyously. "Tolstoy 'just made up' *War and Peace*, you insignificant bugger. Go back to sleep and don't interrupt me or," the pause, "I'll have to ask you to leave the reading."

Theo let his head fall. He rolled his eyes under his lids in an attempt to relubricate them. Behind him, a crash. He turned to see the janitor stack the last chair, save Theo's. He rammed it onto the top of the stack with unnecessary force, glaring at Ott all the while. Then he began sweeping the cleared space, over-clomping his work boots.

". . . so what the hell and what the heck, they swept the house and then went camping, a final attempt to love nature before either it was gone or they were. Lulu was the one who figured out both the tent and the camp stove. Marty angrily stacked firewood. Next morning, they woke in sleeping bag grunge and shrieking clouds of mosquitoes, surrounded by the snoring, still-drunk bodies of local hot-car teens, who used the provincial park for phenomenal parties. Perhaps, Marty thought, they were nature lovers too . . ."

Theo relaxed his muscles and tried not to think about food. He hand-helped himself up and stiff-legged it to the bathroom for a fierce morning pee. The temptation to just carry on into the sunny street was almost impossible to resist. Food. Sleep. Life. His class was beginning in twenty minutes.

But so what. There would be other classes. Other jobs even. You could only beat Ott once.

He returned. He continued to listen and not listen. The janitor shouted something in a foreign language and left, trying but failing to slam the heavy church door. Around noon a gaggle of old people poked their heads in, perhaps to convene a meeting. Ott's now-robotic delivery and lone scowling disciple made short work of them.

Theo had become aware of an interesting part of his mind. It was as if some of it would let go, into delirium or sleep, simply not caring what happened. Thoughts would take off, roiling, jumping, goofy — but strangely knowing. Story lines and rants and scenic descriptions. The oddest part was that for entire minutes he'd be unclear exactly whose voice he was hearing, his own or Ott's.

". . . he tried and tried to find the bird beautiful. To love it. Marty decided that unless he loved it within the next ten minutes, he was going to build a slingshot and kill it . . ."

Theo found himself not so much criticizing Ott's story as adding to it, making it his own. I can do this too, Theo told himself. I can make stuff up too. And, ha ha, I don't even care.

Theo looked quickly up at Ott. That was it. Ott was working hard to stand up, certainly, but he wasn't working at telling his story. He was just telling. And he didn't care.

That was it. Not care. Not work. Just let it go and tell whatever came, just tell, now, as it arrived, as it came in its fresh and bright —

"Would you like to have some breakfast with me?"

Theo went stiff. Very slowly, he lifted his eyes to Ott.

Ott was staring at him. Smiling kindly.

"Would you care to get breakfast at some café?"

Theo closed his eyes and smiled at the world. He stretched his arms wonderfully, glory bursting in every joint.

"Okay," he said. "Sure. It's been quite a long —"

"YES, I WOULD LIKE BREAKFAST, SAID LULU. ANYTHING BUT THESE TENT-BEANS 'N' SHIT WITH SAND IN IT."

Ott's eyes bugged out, full of contempt. He smiled like a panting dog. He enunciated carefully, as if to a child, "If you don't stop interrupting, I'll have to —"

Theo launched himself. He went for Ott's face, but Ott was surprisingly quick, manoeuvring the podium as a shield against Theo's clawed swipes. Ott looked surprised but pleased.

Theo could hear himself actually growling. He might have broken a knuckle on the podium. He didn't care. He wanted Ott. Dragging the podium, backstepping, huffing, the bastard still wouldn't stop talking.

". . . by now, it was clear, Marty didn't like, nature. The tides, the dirt, a cold blast of wind, on his, city-ass, face. Poor schmuck, couldn't take it . . ."

Theo tried kicks at Ott's feet. He smashed his ankle on the podium base.

". . . soon he'd flee, back to civilization, and sterility. Nature would continue without him . . ."

"Shut up!" Theo screamed, hopping, still advancing, holding his ankle. "Shut up!"

". . . without him, without him, without him. Lulu, standing in the wind, outside her tent, wouldn't even remember his name . . ."

"Shut up! Fake!"

". . . Ah, memories of Lulu, memories of the carnal tent, no-holds-barred sweetness and spit . . ."

"Cheat!" Theo shouted, hoarse. "Chimp!"

". . . O sex of rain on the face, O lust of raw food for the famished . . ."

"I know what you're doing!"

Theo suddenly stopped pursuing. Standing, breathing hard, he gave an exaggerated shrug, his palms ending up level with his ears. "It's no big deal, Ott."

Anthony Ott paused where he was. He set the podium upright and leaned on it.

"Marty faces the wind and has an idea," Ott said quietly. He looked intently at Theo, one eyebrow raised.

"Marty's not me," Theo said, approaching, not knowing what he was going to say until he said it. "And Lulu does whatever you tell her to."

"Nope. Too bad. Seems Marty's still trying to think his way out if it." Ott stood his ground as Theo came closer. "Maybe some day he'll be brave enough to tell a story."

"Oh, bullshit, Ott," Theo said through his nose and teeth. They were now face to face, foreheads an inch apart. "I've been telling myself a story all my life . . ."

"Marty's been masturbating in the china cabinet?"

"I don't spew it at everyone. You have no shame."

Nose to nose, Theo could see wild crimson veins on Ott's eyeballs. His eyes were beady and savage, amoral. There was sleep goo in the corners. Theo saw dirty pores, and single hairs coming crazy out of his cheeks. He could smell his breath, coffee and meat and stale liquor.

Looking into Ott's eyes, Theo suffered a strange shift in perception. For a second, he thought he was looking at himself. For a moment, Ott was him. He Ott. It felt wild and frightening, a rude wind building out of nowhere.

"Shame is constipation, said Lulu. And embarrassment is sin." Ott tilted back his head in a pose of grand arrogance. Theo could see up his nostrils.

"Lulu's egomania," Theo found himself saying, "is boring."

Ott brightened. "Shyness turns smart people into dweebs." He leaned forward, pressing his forehead against Theo's. He hissed. "DWEEB."

Theo grabbed Ott's neck and squeezed. "Lulu's gonna die, SAID MARTY."

"Dweeb," Ott croaked. "Thinker. Pick-apart."

They fell to the floor and rolled, Theo still choking Ott.

"Marty squeezed harder," Theo said through his teeth, "and Lulu turned red. The smile fell off her like the leprous wings of a . . ."

"Yeah. Tell a story, Dweeb . . ."

". . . rotting flying dinosaur."

"Fancy pants . . ." Ott could hardly speak.

"Animal."

"Anal . . . brain . . ." Ott's voice trailed off into silence and his eyes closed.

"Pig," whispered Theo. "Child."

Ott said nothing this time. Theo thought he might be dead. Suddenly Ott rolled to the side, out of Theo's hands.

"Nya nya nya nya nyaa nya!"

Ott leapt up and Theo chased him. Gasping, their arms hanging sloppily, they limped around the empty church, Theo following Ott's zigzags. Finding bizarre final energy, Ott tittered like a young girl. Once he stopped, spun to face Theo, and roared like a monster. Theo hesitated a second, and Ott loped away again laughing.

When Ott tried to climb the stage, Theo got a hold of a leg. He pulled Ott, whimpering, to the floor. Again they wrestled, Theo ending up on top.

"It's never gonna stop!" Theo screamed.

"You're right!" Ott screamed back. And then stopped struggling. Both of them gasped for breath. Theo sensed that something was over. Looking into Ott's eyes, which were passive now, he again felt the awful shift, that Ott's eyes were his own.

Ott smiled, and nodded once. For some reason Theo got off. Ott climbed to his feet slowly, helping himself with his hands. He limped to Theo's chair, which had been knocked over. He set it on its legs facing the stage and, groaning, sat down.

"It's your turn," Ott said quietly. He shifted in the chair to get comfortable. He settled, took a breath. Then lifted his face — sober now and all business and frighteningly neutral — to meet Theo's.

"Tell me a story."

HONOURING HONEY

They're not staying the night but Marta wrenches open windows so the cabin airs. Ray is around back turning the water on — she hears the pipes hiss and clank full. Here in the kitchen, her son, Jeff, finally does as he's been asked and gets the broom. Marta waits for him to start sweeping before she speaks.

"Wet it like I told you."

"There's no virus here. You saw the magazine." He doesn't look at her but he has stopped sweeping. He's tall and lanky, wearing his tight white T-shirt, and the bend of his body looks to her like the sound of his whining.

"Wet it."

"Deer mice don't even live around here."

"Wet, the, broom."

Article or no article, there's no telling when a disease might arrive. Marta watches Jeff wet the broom in the sink. She tells him to sweep small, especially if he sees any black rice, which is what they've always called the droppings.

Outside, the rain has stopped. Marta arranges the picnic on the porch table while her daughter, Alison, grumpily wipes down the plastic chairs. Honey lies next to the table, his nose angled way up and nostrils working. For a startling second Marta sees the dog as repellent and alien — it's in the way he's let go of his cloudy old eyes so that his shiny flared nose is the only vital thing about him, a mucousy periscope aimed twitching at the food. Marta looks elsewhere. Overhead, the maples stand in early leaf, their green fresh and tender. This is usually, thinks Marta, the happiest time of year, her secret Thanksgiving, when nature gives itself to her despite her failings. But there, up on the back knoll in sight of everyone, Ray is getting that damnable gun ready, wiping it with a cloth, and Marta wishes he would at least go do that out of sight. He hasn't washed his hair in what looks like days. She doesn't recognize his shirt and hates it, a red-and-black check, a lumberjack shirt. She wonders if, like the rifle, he has borrowed it as well. She hopes not, because that would be just too odd to understand.

Ray keeps getting worse. Honey has become sick again, true, but it doesn't mean you take off work. Honey's pain pills seem to keep him comfortable. All he does is sleep. This morning she found out Ray has taken a leave of absence. They have yet to talk about this. They haven't talked much about anything lately. Ray doesn't listen to a word she says. Asking herself when this began, Marta sees it's tricky to notice a lack of something, especially when it has disappeared over time.

Ray has gone to the car and come back with his fancy bottle of wine. He opens it with the corkscrew he bought too. During the drive he told her the wine had cost thirteen dollars, probably thinking that given the circumstances she would say nothing about the extravagance. He pours it into a yellow plastic cup and takes a taste. He offers it around by lifting the bottle and raising his eyebrows, even to the kids. Marta is glad that no one moves to get any.

This family gathering at the cottage is odd in almost every way, as she predicted it would be. One filet mignon the size of a cupcake is sizzling on the gas barbecue. And everyone brought some sort of mood along. Jeff is supposed to be studying for his Grade 12s, exams that might get him scholarship money. Alison is sulking to find herself out of town away from her boyfriend, Kyle, even for an evening, even though they'd had no plans to be together. During the hour's drive Marta saw the panic under Alison's sulk and realized that her daughter doesn't trust Kyle, and that the breakup would be ugly for everybody.

Ray had insisted. Normally a quiet man, a man you wouldn't notice in a crowd, even this crowd of four, Ray was sarcastic when Jeff tried to beg off due to exams, asking Jeff if he also planned to study the night he, his father, died.

"Can't you wait two weeks?" Jeff asked, with the thin tune of one who's already lost the argument. Ray, a high school teacher, knew the importance of these exams.

"Jeff, *I* can wait two weeks. But Honey's in pain. You want to make *him* wait two weeks? We're talking one evening." Then the final, "Jeff, his love for us is absolute."

Marta knew the questions on the tip of Jeff's tongue — Isn't Honey on painkillers? Can't the vet just do it? — but Ray had answers just as ready. Marta couldn't get a word in either. Maybe Ray hoped that, since he wasn't normally a demanding man, all the years of bending to his family's whims earned him this one stubbornness. But Marta had wanted more of a conversation about it. In the days following his announcement that he wanted to kill their dog himself, explaining that "Honey would want it that way," Marta wanted at least to tell him that Honey couldn't desire any such thing. True, a dog might be more distracted having its family around when it died, but pretending it had human feelings about death was only silly. She wanted Ray at least to admit that this had more to do with what *Ray* wanted. Same with the filet mignon. Why did Ray think a dog contained within it a human version of "the best thing to eat"? How did Ray know Honey's favourite thing wasn't a can of ravioli? She didn't say it, but in her view Honey's favourite food had always been leftover turkey and stuffing.

With a finger, Marta checks the potato salad for coolness. They should be eating it now. She hopes nobody asks for pepper because there isn't any.

Ray leans the rifle — borrowed from one of his firemen friends — against the porch rail, barrel aiming arrogantly at the sky. Marta hopes there's a safety catch of some sort and that it's on. Though what grown child is going to accidently stumble into a rifle? She sees her worry as habit born of the cottage itself and all her summers here, the natural dangers for her babies, then toddlers, then young mischief-makers, who each year ventured farther off this porch. She remembers the first year Honey came here as a pup. She can easily conjure scenes that might bring her to tears. Honey with floppy legs, learning to fetch a pig's ear. A well-skunked Honey sheepish at the door, then the drive to Fatty's Convenience for all their tomato juice. Honey on his blanket in the living room in the deep of night, growling at something outside, warning it away. She can even remember them naming him here, Jeffy scandalized, squealing, "That's a girl's name!" and Ray explaining the honey-colour of the dog's fur and then, pointing at Marta, telling Jeffy, "Mommy calls Daddy 'honey' all the time and is your daddy a girl?" Marta remembers thinking at the time that, since they did often call each other "honey," how odd it was to call their dog that too.

Watching Honey comfortable on the porch, dozing, and flatulent, which has been a problem for them lately, Marta decides to agree with Ray on at least this one, that if they are going to do this themselves then why not here, where Honey had his best times. What better place for a dog? A forest to explore, down the road a lake to swim and frogs to chase and pin; at night a warm cabin and a family to protect. And Marta's always loved it that here at the cabin she didn't have to pick up his messes, except when he uses the badminton area.

Ray passes her without a word and kneels at the dog. He looks close to tears as he attempts a last romp with Honey, teasing him up into a sit with an old tennis ball, asking him if he wants to fetch it. By way of answering, showing what he really wants, one of Honey's eyebrows goes up and he glances at the food table. In the end Ray just pets him briskly. Ray seems much thinner to her, and his hands are too quick in Honey's fur. He looks selfish in what he's doing, like he wants something Honey isn't giving. Marta thinks he wants to cry, is trying to cry but can't. He's using the old baby talk — "Such a *good* puppers. *This* yer nose? *This* yer nose?" — which she finds hard to listen to. As is Jeff, glowering on the porch step. She hears him whisper, "Fucking *hate* this," and he pivots to stare off into the woods, then just as impatiently turns back to catch the rest of his father's performance. More and more, Jeff has his father's cheekbones and dark eyes. She remembers she used to call them bedroom eyes.

Since he's been getting lots of babying lately, Honey is a little bored and he won't let Ray hug and kiss him for long without pulling his head away to give the food table another sniff.

Ray stops caressing him when Alison emerges from the cabin, where she's probably been on the phone with her boyfriend, and from her downcast anger Marta can see that they've had some kind of fight. For whatever reason, Ray decides it's time. He gets off his knees and goes to the rifle. He stands with his fingers lightly on its barrel.

"Anyone wants to watch, come on behind. If not, say your goodbyes. Jeff, I need your help. Bring the steak." He points his chin at the barbecue implements. "Just on that long fork is fine."

Jeff drops his head, hisses "Jesus" to himself, and strides to the barbecue. Marta knows how desperately Jeff wants this to be over. Earlier he had refused to dig the hole for Honey's burial, claiming it was too weird doing it when his dog was still alive and might even limp over to watch. Ray had nodded and apologized, agreeing that it would have been a mistake.

"Bye, Honey," Alison says, sounding like a small girl. Honey turns at his name, tail wagging, but then he sees the steak in the air. Holding the stabbed meat aloft, Jeff says a clipped "Honey" and the dog comes as close to running as he has in weeks, a grotesque hop-and-drag, his front legs being fine, while his back end, which grows both cancer and arthritis, is not.

Alison says "Bye" once more and then she begins to sob. She makes for the cabin but stops and turns back and rushes to hug Marta.

Marta hugs her back firmly. She will not "say her goodbyes." Honey is a dog and does not understand "goodbye," so why say it? But she loves Honey and can barely give him a final glance. When she does watch the dog follow Ray and Jeff behind the cabin, Marta is stricken with the clear sight of his short life span, birth to death, and she can feel it whole in her stomach, which swells sweetly and painfully. She knows it's also the truth of her own death, and her children's too. Oh, poor Honey. Poor all of them.

She decides to try not to blame Ray any more on this subject, no matter how strange he's grown lately, frustrated it seems, maybe what's called mid-life. Lately he's joked about quitting his job and moving to the cabin to be a hermit. Usually he acts up only with his firemen friends — for some reason, three men on their block are firemen — and Ray, falling in with them though they are a decade younger, probably feels he has to prove himself. Last year he herniated a disc skiing behind one of their boats. He has got himself drunk at their parties. He bought a kayak, which he has strapped absurdly to the side of the house, under the eves, to keep dry. To keep a kayak dry! He's been reading books on primitive people and, while she's trying to work at the sink, he tells her about roots that are poisonous unless beaten and soaked in three changes of water. How did these people learn how to do this? he asks her. He's told her that lately he has suffered depression at "what I've done with my life," meaning his teaching career, which admittedly is modest, but doesn't he know he's insulting her job too — she's a receptionist at Sears — as well as insulting her as his wife and this family as his family? Maybe all that time ago she should have let him go back to law school, except she simply had not wanted to raise Ally, then Jeff right after, in starving-student style. But now here's Ray behind the cabin with their Honey and she will dutifully try to change her opinion — a gunshot makes her jump, Alison shouts "*Ow*," and then wails — that Ray has found some old farmer shirt and borrowed a gun *to shoot his dog for show.*

A second gunshot startles her as much as the first. She hopes it means Ray is just making sure, taking no chances on Honey suffering, and not that he botched the first shot. She heard no yelp or sounds of struggle. She won't ask, she doesn't want to hear.

Jeff comes round the corner crying silently. Marta hasn't seen her son's face contorted like this in years, it's her baby's face on a man's big body. It affects her such that she goes to him. Jeff lets her hug him and murmur, "Poor, poor Honey," before he pulls away.

"He hit him right in the eye," Jeff says, then hunches up and cries into his hands.

Ray comes carrying the rifle. Wanting to shout that this is a strange thing he has done, Marta searches his face, which is blank. Perhaps not wanting to be in his father's presence, Jeff goes to the station wagon, for the shovel. His red eyes hate the world.

Ray sits heavily in a white plastic chair. He stares out past his feet.

"That wasn't easy," he says.

Marta doesn't speak. She wishes that what he had just said hadn't sounded so much like a ploy for sympathy. Beside her, Alison doesn't speak either.

He adds in the same monotone, "Well, he's not suffering any more."

Marta sees that Ray, having failed to cry, is taking a different tack.

"Suffering is for the living," he says.

Marta refuses even to nod her head for him. Alison stands aimlessly, then turns to shuffle into the cabin.

"Ally?" Ray says. "Don't phone him quite yet. Let's be a family for a while, okay?"

"I have to go get some Kleenex," she says and goes inside.

"There's just toilet paper," Marta calls after her. "Under the sink."

From below, Jeff shouts, "Here?" Shovel in hand, he is past the old badminton clearing a few steps into the forest, under the big poplar.

Ray points and shouts back, "Way farther away. You'll hit roots there. Ten feet away."

"Here?"

"Yes. Good."

Jeff digs. Alison doesn't return from inside the cabin and Marta suspects she is calling Kyle. Alison should not be disobeying her father, but really how can you blame her?

Ray's fierce clapping of both palms onto both knees startles her.

"Marta. I'm sorry. But I have to."

Marta waits for him to continue and when all he does is shake his head at the floor, she asks, "Have to what?"

"Don't be upset, okay? But I'm going to. See it as — It's honouring Honey. An animal would understand *exactly this*."

"What, Ray?" Something in the shakiness of his manner makes her stomach hollow.

"Well, I'm — Please, just listen. You never listen to me. Just listen, okay? And I'm not sure I want the kids to know, but I want you to know — I'm going to eat Honey. I'm going to eat *some* of him." Ray opens his nostrils in taking a big gulp of wine. He takes another one, finishing the yellow cup, tilting his head back and looking up into the sky.

Marta wants to say "Are you serious?" when it's plain to her that serious is all he is.

"I want to eat his — Don't be upset, it's really not that strange, but I think I'm going to eat his heart. If I can find it." He smiles like this last bit is a joke she would want to enjoy with him.

"Ray, not that you're serious, but no."

"Marta? In other cultures, it's the biggest honour. Honey would —"

"Stop." Marta thrusts one hand out, blocking sight of him. "Don't joke about it, Ray."

"Not joking about it." Ray gently shakes his head while gazing at his feet, as though afraid to look at her. "It's the best thing anybody can do. Other cultures, they eat the heart of their, their *enemies*, it's how — it's a way of, of taking in the best — it's ultimate *respect*, it —"

"I'm not listening, Ray." For some reason, Marta puts her hands over her eyes.

"Well, you never do listen, Marta. I want you to listen now. Honey was — Honey was the best thing that —".

"Ray, you're scaring me now."

"It's how much I love Honey. I want to show it."

"Ray, to who? Who do you want to show it to?"

"I mean, even just a piece, just a taste. It's symbolic, Marta."

"What, you going to barbecue him?" She glares at the barbecue, which is still ticking from the filet mignon, a few shreds of dark meat stuck to the grill.

"Just a piece. If I can't find the heart right away. The kids don't have to know."

"Ray. I'm serious now. I know you've felt frustrated but this isn't funny."

Ray almost growls, "*Who says it's funny?*" and Marta has to look at him. "Honey is dead. He's been —" Now Ray's eyes are showing something to her, it's a cruel light he knows is there. "He's the closest thing to love I've had in eleven years, Marta."

"Ray? Please? Listen to me?"

"I always listen to you. You never listen to me. Still aren't."

"Well, Ray? I don't even know who you think you're talking to right now."

"Honey kept this family together for eleven years, you know that? He was the only one who cared about anything except himself."

"How much have you had to drink?" Marta stares at the bottle she can see is nearly full.

"I want to eat him, Marta!"

"No you don't."

"Honey would want me to!"

"Honey is a dog! Honey is a dead dog! Honey doesn't want anything!"

Ray begins to cry now in a shocking way, eyes open, looking straight at her. Marta's hair rises when she understands that he is crying not for Honey but because he isn't getting his way.

Ray coughs, softens, and looks over at their son. He sighs deeply, glances back at Marta, and shrugs. He lurches to his feet and announces, "Well, Alison's talking to her boyfriend and Jeff's digging a hole, so I better get a knife."

He steps soberly into the cabin. Marta watches the doorway for a moment, half-hoping Ray will pop out grinning, slap his knee, and point at her, but she knows he won't. When he reappears he will have that same blank face, and a knife. Marta even knows what knife.

Marta goes for the rifle, grabbing it by the barrel. Though it's heavy this way she holds it out from herself, disgusted. She walks it down the porch steps. On her way to the car, a hand cupping one side of her mouth, shielding her words from the cabin, she calls, "Jeff!"

"What." Jeff wipes his brow with a forearm. He has been digging in a huff and a blister on his palm is bleeding. He doesn't look at her.

"Come here, now. We're going."

"Dad wanted it four feet. It's only two. It's not even two."

"Leave it. We're going. Right now."

"I have to finish Honey's hole."

"Your father wants you to leave. *Right now.*"

"But we can't just —"

"*Now.*"

Marta hears Jeff swear as she wrenches up the station wagon's trunk and lays the gun on the dog blanket. She realizes that what she is smelling is burnt gunpowder, from the bullets that shot Honey. Jeff said Ray fired one right into Honey's eye. What kind of love is that? Now Jeff is beside her, trying to angle the shovel in. Ray had somehow got it to fit for the drive out.

"Fine," says Jeff, trying to force the shovel in. Marta is afraid he might clunk a window.

"Leave it. Leave it here for your father." Marta points at the ground, but Jeff doesn't drop it. He looks at her cautiously.

"Your father and I have had a fight, Jeff. He's going to stay here. I want you to go get Alison and tell her that your father and I have had a fight and that I am driving away in this car in no more than thirty seconds. Otherwise, she is staying here with your father. And —"

"But why isn't —"

"— And I want you to *run.*"

Jeff shakes his head, mumbling, as he half-runs to the cabin.

Very likely, Marta knows, Jeff thinks she's crazy too. She gets in and starts the car. She backs onto the badminton area, puts the car in drive, and edges out so it points at the road. What will she do if Ray comes after them, waving his hands for her to stop? Apologizing in front of the children. If that happens she doesn't know what she'll do. But she doubts they'll see any of that. When she gets home, what she will do is phone one of those firemen of his, tell him what Ray has done. Firemen know emergencies, they might have some advice. They might agree that it was just showing off, which is what men do. Honouring Honey? Shooting her like he's some farmer? Ray teaches high school. Ray is nothing but the most ordinary of men. But now he's showing off, he's walking on his hands, and she is not going to watch.

In the rearview Marta sees Jeff and Alison come at a trot. Did Ray say anything to them?

Two car doors open and close behind her and Marta steps on the gas, the tires spinning on the moss and dirt, which is hard not to do in any case. She takes a breath then announces, "Your father is going to have a little holiday here by himself." Neither child answers her. The car is moving and she is more afraid than she should be — and there he is now, framed in the rearview, there is Ray. Of course he is aware of them leaving, of course he hears the car. He doesn't seem to care. He is not lurching or crying like a madman but instead he crosses the porch in a few ordinary steps, pointing the carving knife safely down, if anything looking content as he rounds the corner to get at Honey.

The station wagon crunches down the lane, through trees that are almost too close even for one car, the crooked branches reaching for her, and when the tires finally hit pavement, the suddenly cool and smooth sound puts everything that just happened back into another time and place. Marta sighs, then works to breathe routinely. She finds her children in the rearview and is glad to see that Alison's face is already full of Kyle, though Jeff's is disgusted with his father. And perhaps with her. She can change that. She will tell them what she has understood, that their father has stepped over the line this time, and that if he ever expects to sleep in her house again they will have to have a talk, and he will have to listen.

Mercurial

POINT NO POINT

Neil McRae puts his suitcase down and says, mindlessly but sincerely, "Great!"

Joanne places hers beside Neil's. Both gaze out the picture window at the famous oceanview that this evening is obscured by a perfectly uniform press of fog. Tomorrow is the longest day of the year, the solstice, and Neil wonders if they'll see it. Their daughter, Vicky, has trailed them in, pulling her suitcase-on-wheels, chewing fresh gum. Neil can smell mint behind him.

"Unbelievable," Vicky says. "You were right, no TV."

Joanne stabs her finger at the window. "That's the *best* TV."

"A two-hundred incher," says Neil, trying to lighten things. It'll take time for travel jitters to fade. He'd love to grab a beer from that little fridge but of course it's empty, which is a problem he'll tackle tomorrow. On the long bus ride here he noticed the endless giant trees and complete absence of stores but he'll keep this to himself. Joanne's already mad at herself for screwing up connections — two buses and waiting rooms took five hours to get them maybe eighty miles, whereas the flight all the way from Calgary to Victoria had taken just one. Joanne hadn't let Neil rent a car. It was Joanne's retirement, and if she wanted to waste five hours on buses it was her choice.

"So this counts as the first day?" Vicky asks. She hasn't dropped her suitcase handle. At first Vicky was going to stay home alone, but after her delivery to the front door by the cops a month ago, arrangements were made for her to stay with Joanne's bowling partner Raquel, who in the past two weeks has fallen seriously ill. When Vicky learned she had to come with them she began moaning, "Five *days*." Neil saw only that she didn't complain about them not trusting her to stay on her own, which to his mind proves them right.

"This was day one," says Joanne encouragingly, willing to be happy for her daughter but the slope to her voice letting them know she is sad for herself.

"Check out the goat on the driver?" Neil asks them. He is at the sink testing the cold, then the hot, taps. The fixtures are solid but not what you'd call elegant. He holds his finger under until the stream warms, then he turns it off. By "goat" he means goatee.

"I didn't, no," says Joanne.

"He was a kid. It's coming back."

Neil grew his goatee forty years ago when he was twenty, the kind favoured by Wolfman Jack and, for a while, the Philadelphia Flyers. And of course bikers everywhere, and Neil has always had his Harley. Jet black and thick, his goatee is an extension of the head of hair he used to style in glossy waves, a style a friend said could hide a crow. Employees at Neil's hardware store always told customers with queries to see the man with the goatee.

Joanne leans in and whispers, "She's taking our room."

Vicky has wandered into the larger bedroom and swings her suitcase up onto the bed, which looks to be bigger than the one in the smaller room.

Joanne has Neil by the arm. "Don't. Let's all just relax."

"Brochure said there's a bar. Think they sell off-sale? And we can ask about groceries."

"Well, we can eat at the restaurant."

"It said 'fine dining.' Did we remortgage?"

He's smiling but Joanne answers seriously, in charge. It's her vacation. She says, "We can treat ourselves a few times."

"There's a whole little *box* of chocolates on my pillow," Vicky calls from their bedroom.

Next morning in the lodge they stand first in line at the dining room's entrance, which is blocked by a plum-velvet rope strung between bronze-cupid posts, the kind of thing you'd see in an old movie house, and which looks funny in all this cedar and glass. Vicky won't stand with them, hissing, "You're not supposed to 'line up.'" True, they're the only ones in line, but they're starving. Neil explains that since they're from Alberta they're an hour hungrier than all the other folks here. Who do look to be from the West Coast. Men in sandals, women wearing no makeup and almost colourless clothing that still comes off looking expensive. Some women are alone or in groups, women (whispers Joanne) who might be professors. On their walk to the lodge they noticed it was all B.C. and two Oregon cars parked in front of the cabanas, lots of Volvos and late model Hondas and one of those new electric hybrids, not popular in oily Alberta. It's the first hybrid car Neil has seen in person, and he pointed and said, "In Drumheller we'd shoot that." Their cabana is the only one without a car out front.

Eventually a sleepy-looking young man unhooks the velvet from cupid's elbow and mumbles while walking away that they can sit anywhere.

The dining room is all windows, all of them bright with solid fog. Joanne declares it beautiful, gazing around as if the windows offer some variety. Neil wonders aloud if they could see the beach from here, and then reminds himself not to complain, and to be glad he's here.

When Neil retired and sold the hardware store he flew to Cincinnati by himself. What drew him was an article about a TV Museum. The old TVs and the '50s living-room replicas he described to Joanne as "sweet and sour," meaning it made you feel too old and young at the same time. He couldn't explain to her exactly why he spent all those hours there just watching the shows — *F-Troop, Combat!, Queen for a Day* — but when he got home he felt the trip had been a good one and he had no regrets about not seeing more sights, or a Reds game.

So he felt humbled when, though only fifty-three, Joanne decided to retire now too and announced that the only retirement trip she could imagine included him. That Vicky was a last-minute addition was sad, for Joanne had been planning for two years, talking it up endlessly, and Neil joked that it sounded like they were really going to Eden.

What first twigged Joanne to the Point No Point area, and EdenTides Resort, was a Sears co-worker who returned from a vacation there. Joanne didn't particularly like Dorothy but you don't ignore a person who speaks with such passion about a place. Then one day Joanne thumbed through a book called

North America's Sacred Spots and there was Point No Point again, being called "a zone of powerful silence." The name came from a land form that looked like a point but wasn't.

For two years Neil watched Joanne read about British Columbia and solstice-this and healing-that. He stopped ribbing her, because why not get excited about something? Even if it meant planning a vacation around a solstice? At their age, excitement was harder to come by. And he was a bit excited himself at seeing whales, and possibly a bear. But Neil noticed with a snicker how Joanne acted the instant they left Drumheller, as if they were already somewhere great and everything was worth mentioning. In Calgary she was pointing out things on the way to the airport — an old gas station, an African restaurant, and a yard with probably twenty cheap gnomes in it.

Their eggs benedict (on yam muffin with smoked salmon) arrive. When Neil calls the waiter back to get some extra butter, Vicky smiles, stares down at her tapping fork, and asks the young man, "So what's there to do around here?"

The waiter stops, gives her a look, and says, "Hmmm" like he's assessing her and will tailor his answer. Neil doesn't like his manner — the little smile, the drum roll on his belt buckle — not because he's eyeing his daughter but because he's getting paid to be a waiter so that's what he should be. He looks like the kind of boy who recently had a ponytail but now doesn't. He greeted them here at the table by saying, "Happy solstice," and Neil couldn't figure his attitude.

"Well, we're having a bonfire tonight," he says to Vicky like Neil's not even here. "Might be okay. Few people just hangin'."

"What," asks Vicky softly, "just down here?" She drifts a thumb over her shoulder at the ocean unseen but dully loud beyond the windows. Her half-smile Neil knows is meant to look superior.

"That's the resort beach. We're at the next one over."

He tells her to stop by at eight and he'll walk with her there. His name is Alex, and his parents "sort of own this place."

Vicky asks Alex more questions, not letting him go get the extra butter, which Neil knows will be forgotten altogether. He lets his face fall into cupped hands. He can't pretend he isn't tired. Last night Joanne did get Vicky to switch rooms, and she was embarrassed for eating the little box of chocolates meant for them. But the bed was hard in that way that's supposed to be good for you and he had an awful sleep, though he always slept awful in strange beds — it had happened in Cincinnati too. Undressing, Joanne raised eyebrows and dangled black negligee from pinched fingers, but they both agreed they would "use it" another night. Joanne had bought the negligee for herself a year ago. In truth, Neil wasn't eager to "use it." Her body looked nothing like it did thirty years ago. He didn't mind her tubbiness down there, but you really don't want it framed.

Vicky asks Alex the waiter why this place is called Point No Point and Neil is surprised she even noticed.

"If you're out on a boat," the waiter says quickly, used to this one, "*approaching*, it looks like you're rounding a point that just keeps going and going and it isn't a point at all. It's sort of an optical illusion."

At this the waiter clicks his heels together and speeds away. Neil calls "Butter?" to his back, which causes him to spin in a full circle, falsely smiling.

Not ten seconds pass before Vicky joins her father with face-in-hands and she asks again what there is to do here.

Joanne is ready. She shakes her head. "Vicky? We came here to sit still and breathe."

Vicky does sit down with a pile of magazines in the lodge fireplace area so Neil and Joanne head back for showers. En route they pass an odd, tall woman with long grey hair who looks like she would be shy in the city but here she wishes them happy solstice.

Waiting for his turn in the tub Neil stares out the window into the hanging white. He's learned the fog is normal but that there's a chance of it breaking today and their view coming out. He picks up the brochure, more the size of a book, looking for Services, but there aren't any. Instead there are paragraphs about *not* having services, not even phones or TVs or radios, and instead you got silence and healing and raccoons visiting your porch. There are pages on local arts and crafts, with pictures of pottery. There's a page on the Indians who once lived here, and one on Spanish explorers (which is why islands are Galiano and Cortes), and how Captain Vancouver came to map the area for England, and gave Point No Point its name. There's a page on the "resident" bald eagles, and ravens, which are described not as "tricksters" but as "The Trickster." All interesting, but to Neil, who was in business for thirty-three years, it rings suspiciously like fancy excuses for why a bare-bones resort costs so much.

He listens to Joanne showering, hearing changes in spray that mean she's reaching for shampoo or enjoying a blast on the neck. He Frisbees the brochure onto the table. Amazing they are finally here. Here they are. The place she's talked about for so long. One plan had been to go to Sally Too's, the main art gallery for local artists. "Artists from around the world,"

Joanne told him, more than once, "choose to live here." Thing is, he's just read that Sally Too's is fifteen miles down the road and there will be no getting there without a car, another thing Neil will keep to himself and hope Joanne doesn't discover.

Showers done, it's decided Neil will do the grocery run while Joanne hikes off on the trails, the main activity here. Neil suggests this arrangement, reminding her of his solo adventure to Cincinnati and hinting how it might be good for her to do the first hike alone, because it's her retirement and this is her special place. She dresses against the chill of the fog, throwing a bright yellow scarf around her neck. She's so excited that as she strides out the door when he wishes her good luck she can barely mumble a reply.

Neil finds no good luck himself. He spends the afternoon seeking some sort of ride to the nearest grocery, which is in Sooke, a half-hour back along the curvy road. The one bus was hours ago. A taxi is a hundred bucks. They really should have planned better but Neil just wants to get the fridge filled, find some beer and wine, make a nice meal for her. Steaks, a fancy salad with sliced eggs in it.

Maybe because it's Sunday, or because of wild solstice parties or whatever the hell they do here, no one at the Sooke taxi answers. Now the guy at the lobby desk is impatient with him hogging the phone. The guy — Andrew — hesitated shaking hands when Neil stuck his out and said, "Neil McRae, cabin fourteen." Andrew didn't smile once, making Neil want to call him Andy, and he had nothing more helpful to say than, "We *do* have an excellent restaurant." He says this twice, which Neil decides is a sort of insult.

Out in the parking lot he considers hitchhiking but suspects that a burly older man standing in fog on a gravel shoulder with his thumb out looks like bad luck. The goatee makes him look even riskier. And though he stopped the weights a decade ago he knows he can still look dangerous in a T-shirt, especially the tight blacky he has on now. Not knowing what to do, he sees a younger man in jeans taking a white bucket out of the trunk of his tan Mercedes.

"How ya doing there?" Neil says to be friendly, but mostly to let the guy know he's a fellow patron of the resort, not someone who's considering hitchhiking to Sooke for beer.

"I'm doing *well*. Found a nice appetizer." He tilts the bucket at Neil. Black shells.

"Watcha got there?"

"Oh, a good bunch of mussels," says the man, quite proud. "Steam 'em in wine and garlic — *oh* yes."

"Get 'em yourself?"

"You have to hunt a little but they're around. Any low tide. Go that way, or that way" — He points either direction along the highway — "Find a road down to the beach, find a rock outcrop. Find a fissure in the rock, they cluster in there. You need a heavy knife or screwdriver or something, pry them off." He makes prying motions with one hand and he grits his teeth.

"Okay, thanks, that sounds good."

"The tide's still good right now. I found a road down, five miles south of here."

"Well, great. I think I will."

"And the red tide's okay. I phoned Fisheries. The PSP update."

"Oh yeah?"

"Which is so reassuring."

"It sure is."

"So, wine and garlic, ten minutes, maybe some lemon as well, dip some baguette in the broth or, or — do know what's *good*?"

"No."

"*Foccacia*. Dip some foccacia. *Oh* yes. With the salt, the embedded rock salt."

"Well, okay. I'll do that."

"Good luck."

"Hey, thanks." Neil is already turning away when out the side of his face he adds, "Happy solstice," feeling bad even as he says it, but the man with the Mercedes calls back, "Yes!"

Out behind the lodge Neil finds and empties a white compost pail. He grabs the sturdiest knife from his kitchenette drawer. Joanne still hasn't returned — she must be having herself a time. He heads down the trail into the fog, through the trees, some really humongous trees, they really are big. Paths crisscross but it's easy — just keep heading downhill where the water's going to be. The surf grows louder and louder the closer he gets.

It's good to be out of the trees, and on the beach it's fairly exciting. It lies under the canopy of fog and he can see not only the waves crashing on shore but also across the water to a distant wall of black that, according to the map, is Washington State, several miles away. Here on the beach it feels ten degrees colder, hard to believe it's almost July, and Neil finds himself striding to a rock outcrop with tight, herky-jerky speed. He should have grabbed his leather vest.

It doesn't take long. In fact, this beach is mostly rock outcrop and there are mussels galore, clustered in the fissures, sure, but also spilling out in carpets of nothing but mussels. Neil simply stoops and begins scraping a cluster away. It takes no time at all. No need to drive anywhere. Odd that no one's discovered this spot, right here at the base of the main path to the resort, and a resort with kitchenettes no less.

He keeps it neat, carving out a square patch, maybe four feet by four feet, on the mussel-covered rock face. Mussels are really quite something, so black and glossy, way more exotic than your basic clams. Turn them in the light and they shine hints of blue, just like a crow. And now the bucket is full. Neil hefts what feels like six, seven pounds of mussels — plenty for dinner, and just in time. Heading up the trail back into the forest, he wonders if he likes mussels. He's pretty sure he had them in Calgary once, at that hardware conference. He knows they're orange, which is a weird colour meat to put in your mouth.

Her crying starts that evening.

Neil returns from his food mission with a bucket of mussels, a bottle of what he's been told is good B.C. white wine, and French bread. He even has a plastic baggie of butter pats. After complaining to Andy the desk guy that their brochure fails to mention there being no stores anywhere, Andrew let him buy some wine from the bar at cost after Neil agreed to tell no one, since it was "highly illegal." Neil didn't care for his churchy way of doing business, like there's something wrong with you for wanting wine in the first place. Neil begged some bread too, and at the door he remembered butter. He hated bread without butter, it was one of his little things, as Joanne called them. Throw in some of those butter pats and you have yourself a deal, he joked, the joke being that, with wine in hand and paid for, the deal was already done. Andy didn't smile, and for this and other reasons Neil was now pretty certain he was the owner, which would make him that waiter's father. Not that it was "a deal" anyway — fifteen bucks for one skinny bottle of wine. Stepping out into the fog and aiming himself at his cabin, Neil thumbed the bottle neck through the plastic bag to make sure it wasn't a screw-top.

He comes in whistling, loaded down with their romantic dinner, and Joanne is curled on the couch bucking with sobs. She hears him and keeps crying as she looks up, cheeks wet and shiny, eyes red but wide open and just looking at him. And the slightest, scariest smile.

"Where's Vicky?" is what Neil automatically says.

But Joanne shakes her head and says Vicky's fine, Vicky's been in and out, she gave her money for the evening and made her promise to act responsibly. It's not Vicky, Joanne says.

She says she doesn't know what it is. She adds, "I'm fine," before coughing into sobs again. Neil grabs her up and hugs her timidly. He asks if something happened. Before shaking her head she hesitates, which scares him. He has no idea how to hug her or for how long. He tries, "I know you miss Sears, hon, but this is ridiculous," and she can't even laugh. So he holds her until she settles and he hears another, "I'm fine." Then she bravely asks him what he's brought.

Neil explains his day, and promises to make a proper grocery run tomorrow. He tells her you really do need a car here. Joanne nods at this and for a second he thinks he's triggered more tears, but she takes an interest and goes to look in the bucket in the sink. He tells her his idea, which is to melt half the butter pats for dipping, but save the rest for the bread. He asks if she likes mussels and she's unsure.

"We'll steam them up in that wine," says Neil. "They're good that way."

Joanne whimpers, waking him. She scrambles out of bed and Neil goes up on an elbow. Her timing, why now? He is frightened anew, speechless watching her moaning dance. At her most tearful surges she smacks her bare feet on the cabana's pine floor, trying to make noise. Her new black lingerie rides high on her, rumpled from their sex and dark wet at the belly. It did make her look silly and older and Neil feels nothing but bad to think this about her now, as if these thoughts of his can reach her through the air and add to her horrible burden. Whatever it is. He only half-understands what she told him, and he still wants to try to find a doctor.

Slapping at the air, she spins around, sees him watching.

"Neil, oohh, I'm just — I don't —"

She seems worse. She stares fiercely at him then punches the heels of her palms into her mouth. Her cheeks puff in and out as she breathes and she gazes off now at nothing, looking truly crazy. He has come to understand while watching her tonight that, when you no longer care what you look like to others, there's no question you're in some sort of trouble, and for Joanne, so careful with her looks, this is twice as true.

"Ohh!" Joanne throws her head back and this leads her in a stumble to the couch where she flops. She closes her mouth tight and forces long hissing breaths through her nostrils.

Neil has struggled up, got his pyjamas back on, and stoops at her side, not quite touching her with his outstretched hand.

"Sweetheart? Sweetheart, is there pain? Can you — can you feel something? Physically wrong?"

Joanne shakes her head.

"If there is I want to call a doctor." He adds, almost as a threat, "I'm calling a doctor anyway." He's said all this before, several times.

"*Neil!*" She flings her hands toward his face to stop him talking. She turns to escape him, sees something worse out the dark window, and plunges her face into the cushions to escape that too. She gathers cushions around her head. Her whimpering is muffled but Neil hears words in it. He bends lower to catch what might give him some clue.

He hears, "I told you. I told you what it is. I told you, I told you."

Sure, she did. He still doesn't know what to make of it. Over dinner — a half hour of no crying at all — she told him she was walking when it happened, when *something* happened. She had just climbed up from the beach, the famous wilderness beach, which had all been exactly as described, perfect. The towering old growth cedar and hemlock, the whispering breeze up in their canopy, which speaks to you. She heard a raven — it croaked at her, then clucked. She maybe saw a whale breach, a huge splash off in the distance. A couple she spoke to had yesterday seen an orca. Yes, it was Eden. In fact, as soon as she'd set foot on the beach she had thanked the place. She had said out loud to the ocean, not feeling silly at all, "Thanks for bringing me here. You were right." Everything was perfect, and wonderful. And then, back on the trail, it happened. She stopped dead in the middle of the gorgeous trail, she looked around her, and panicked. She couldn't catch her breath and she started shaking. Shaking, crying, holding on to a tree for support.

When she told Neil the problem, none of it made sense to him. One thing she said was, "I knew it was all over." *No*, she didn't mean she was sad to be retired, and getting old. It wasn't that at all. Another thing she said was, "I knew that this was it, there was nothing better than this." To Neil's question, "So you *do* like it here then?" she got angry and told him that she loved it here and that was the problem. He tried suggesting that she was overtired, which made her cry harder in frustration. He asked her if, after all the build-up, she was maybe having a little let-down? *Yes!* she said. A *big* let-down. But didn't she just say she liked it here? Yes, *and there's nothing left!*

Though dinner was thick with this kind of talk, and Neil hardly noticed the mussels going into his mouth, Joanne said it was the best dinner she'd ever had. Neil said some garlic would have been nice, and more wine, but — look out there, the fog was gone and the stars were out. Which for some reason set her off crying again.

Sex was her idea. Because of this and her general spookiness he was nervous, but he rose to it. There was crying in the middle, then an awkward attempt to start it up again, which somehow worked, for both of them, but then there was crying, way more crying, at the end.

And more now. It's the middle of the night. He needs to fix this. His hand on her shoulder, which has stopped convulsing for the moment, he decides to try to get her talking again, though it sometimes triggers the crying.

"So, Joanne, so, Joanne, honey, are you saying that you think there's nothing left to live for? I think there's lots left to live for. There's a ton. There's way more great places to see."

She answers him and he drops to his knees to hear her say through the cushions, "Neil, I know. It's not that."

He has an idea. "Are you thinking you maybe want to *move* here?"

"No I don't think so. I don't think that would —"

"Because we could." He shouldn't be saying this but he senses new interest under those cushions. "If, if that's what you want. Another couple years, Vicky's not so much in the picture and —"

"Vicky. Go check on Vicky."

Neil flicks on the hallway light and silently turns the doorknob to Vicky's room. He can't hear her breathing so he leans in further, to see. He closes her door and returns to the couch to sit beside Joanne, who has knocked away the cushions and is staring at the ceiling.

"Yeah, she's fine."

"What time is it?"

"Three. Ten past three."

"No, I couldn't move here," she says. And, after a moment, "I don't fit."

"Well, then it's not good enough for you."

Neil doesn't wonder, not for a moment, if that might be true. All he sees is, for the moment she isn't crying, and she no longer looks on the verge of crying, and maybe whatever happened to her is gone. But her face says differently and there's no way he's going to tell her that Vicky's not in her room. It's like he couldn't tell her even if he wanted to. He feels pulled in two directions, by two women he somehow no longer knows.

The next morning, getting dressed for brunch in the restaurant, Neil pokes his head in Vicky's room and pretends to be surprised, telling Joanne, "Hey — she's already up and out." And now in the restaurant — the velvet rope is down so they just wander in and take a table — Neil and Joanne see their daughter approach wearing an apron with an EdenTides logo. She has menus, a pad and pencil, and a deadpan joke going.

"Good morning, I'm Victoria and I'll be your waitress this morning?" Not breaking a smile she places the menus and jots on her pad. She chirps, a bit deliriously, "And you're table *one*?" Neil doesn't know what to say and Joanne has an eyebrow way up. "Alex," Vicky tells them in a stage whisper, notepad over her mouth, "had a rough night. I'm doing his shift."

Neil can see her nervousness through all this, her waiting for the explosion, like the one a month ago. Across the table Joanne looks troubled again, staring but not seeing, like someone doing hopeless math in her head.

Neil asks his daughter, "Do you know how?"

Vicky cocks a hip and readies herself to write in her pad. "Would you like extra butter with that bread, sir?"

"Hey, you do. You're good."

"Do you *mind* doing this?" Joanne asks, sincere as Neil has ever seen her. Damned if she isn't going to cry again.

"Alex told me ten an hour plus tips."

Neil asks, "How about Andrew?"

"Who's Andrew?"

"I think he owns this place."

"Alex's dad?"

"Thin guy, glasses, yeah."

"His dad's not . . . saying much. When Alex shows up I'll remind him he said ten plus tips."

"Okay." Neil cracks open his menu and peers in. "What's the special?"

"Sockeye in an omelette with chipotle. It's very fresh."

"I don't know what that is," Neil says, "but you're good."

"I'm *really* good," Vicky says as she curls away.

Neil mumbles "butter" to Joanne and rises to chase his daughter. Around the corner at the double door to the kitchen he catches her by the arm. She spins, won't look him in the eye.

"Your mother doesn't know." He squeezes harder. "Don't tell her."

Vicky looks up. Though no one's in hearing range she

mouthes an over-large *thank you*. Neil sees her bloodshot eyes, her fatigue. He releases her and she turns quickly and shoulders through the door into the kitchen.

"Butter," Neil tells Joanne again when he returns.

"She has your sense of humor," Joanne says, not looking up from the menu.

Scanning his for sausages, spotting none, Neil weighs this. He did find her waitress routine funny. "Well, I guess maybe she does."

After a time Joanne says, "I hope Alex learned a lesson." She seems to have figured the math out in her head.

"She looks good in that getup," Neil says. It's true. She's showered — she's had herself a shower somewhere — and looks fresh. Her shirt is buttoned all the way up, and not a wrinkle in that apron. Sometimes his daughter can look slutty, and though it's how they all look these days he doesn't like it. Despite the night, this morning she looks good, a good employee.

"Anyway, Neil" — Joanne puts her hand over his — "I'm feeling better. You helped." She pauses, pulls her hand away. "I know what happened now. I healed. I had to heal, and I did."

He really hopes it's true that she's better. He thinks he's tearing up now himself. He's so tired. This vacation has been . . . like some sort of trial. He directs his gaze out the window. The fog is thinner. There's wind in there swirling it around. He doesn't like this place.

"Hey," he says, "you haven't had a good cry like that in a while."

"No, I guess I haven't."

"So you're feeling better."

"Let's play cards tonight. Let's get a deck of cards. And *two* bottles of wine."

"Two. Holy cow."

"I'm on vacation."

"Yes you are."

"I'm retired."

"Welcome to the *big* vacation, then."

"Thank you."

Joanne lifts her water glass and so does Neil. They clink them. He finds her eye, and there she is, it's her. There's that confidence she has when she gets the high bowling score, or sometimes when she comes home from church.

"So, was that some of that *super* menopause I was warned about?" He chuckles, and she blinks rapidly and looks out the window. "Sorry, sorry — that was some of my famous sense of humour."

"It's okay."

"Sorry. Can we do this again?" He raises his water glass, but she doesn't. Instead she asks him to remind her to phone Raquel, who had her scan yesterday.

Vicky comes for their orders and both want the sockeye special. Neil asks Vicky if she wouldn't mind checking what the house dressing is and Vicky says yes and thanks him, saying it's something she should know. Neil is just beginning to feel okay about things, about his wife not crying any more and his daughter doing a good job, when the desk guy — Andrew, the owner — appears at their table, breathing heavily. He almost shoulders Vicky out of the way. His face is so slack it takes a second for Neil to realize the man is angry.

"Was it you," Andrew begins, catching his breath. "Was it you, who took those mussels, down in front?"

"Yesterday? Down here?" Neil points at the window.

"From the resort beach — was that you?"

Trying a little half-smile, Neil looks up to face him. He is aware of a table of ladies, and his daughter and his wife, paying close attention.

"Hey, we wanted some, you know, some *solstice*-mussels. There a problem?"

"Can you read?"

"Can you *run*?"

Joanne's hard hand pins his to the table, and the guy asks if that was some kind of threat. Neil can feel his leather vest tight over his grey T-shirt, which is tight as well. His heart is going pretty good. He hasn't been in a fight in too many years.

Andrew jabs his finger and hisses, way too loud, that the brochure explains clearly, as does the laminated card on the back of the bathroom door, that no harvesting of shellfish is allowed on the property, just as guests are not to pick wildflowers or — and here the guy's hiss becomes a shout — "*chop down the bloody trees for firewood.*" He asks if Neil even noticed what he "brutalized," that there's now an ugly square of bare rock, "ruining a pristine beach that is no different than a garden."

Neil speaks softly. "This is my wife, Joanne." He shakes a finger at her. "It's her retirement vacation." He glances at her, expecting to see her in tears again, expecting at least an expression that will help his point and make this guy Andrew feel bad. He is surprised to see her clear-eyed, looking almost bored, like what's happening here at their table is nothing much.

"And — and this is my daughter, Vicky, doing your son's job. Maybe when he gets out of bed you can get him to, you know, glue a bunch of mussels from someone else's beach back onto yours." Using only his nostrils to breathe, Andrew widens his eyes at this but he doesn't move. Neil sees that his glasses are dotted with salt spray and that the knees of his pants are wet. This guy has been down on the beach, really upset about his rock.

"Okay, no, seriously," Neil continues, trying actually to be helpful now, because the guy is still just staring, and hasn't been thinking straight, what with his kid out all night too. "If you took all the *rest* of the mussels off that, you know, rock outcrop, it would look better. Really, it would look okay. It would be, you know, 'uniform.'" Andrew is still staring. "I could give you a hand. Hey, you could add them to the menu. A mussel special. You know, they're pretty good if you steam them in a little wine."

He turns to the window. Above are drifting cuts of blue, and he can see down through moving gaps to distant black water, not unlike the view from a landing plane. The remaining fog seems to be churning in fear of the sun. He has just been given public shit and is embarrassed at having been friendly in return. He hopes the guy knows he has been let off easy.

But Andrew, who only now identifies himself as the owner of EdenTides Resort, quietly tells the three of them that he won't instigate criminal charges, or enforce the specified $500 vandalism fine, or charge them for the two nights, or for this brunch. He does insist that he and his family vacate the premises as soon as they finish their meal.

"You get paid?"

Hair dripping from the shower, Vicky is getting her suitcase-on-wheels together.

"I sure did."

"Atta girl." Neil is glad she doesn't mention the twenty tip he left her. "It's good you finished your shift. Mom says you even went in back and helped with clean-up."

Vicky says it was the most passive-aggressive thing she could think of and Neil has only a fleeting sense of what his daughter might mean. Nor does he know what to make of what he overheard her telling her mother, when Joanne asked if she'd seen Alex today and Vicky told her with a sassy little smile, "I left him crying beside the walk-in fridge."

But Neil is proud how no one in his family lost their cool in the face of hostility. Joanne is off on the trails having a last little hike, in the sun. And Neil has some business of his own still to attend to. Their taxi won't be here for another half hour.

When it does come, Vicky gets up front with the driver, who introduces himself as Chris. He pivots awkwardly and shakes Neil's and Joanne's hands. In the air is that it's going to be a long ride.

As they begin taking the curves, Neil watches Joanne closely. She's alert and smiles at all the sights they pass. He no longer knows this woman.

"Have a nice walk?"

"It was wonderful."

"Nicer in the sun?"

"Still cold by the water but it wakes you up."

Neil calls forward, "Ever get warm here, Chris?"

"Nope."

"Well, *that* sucks." He waits. "I'd say that place sort of sucked in general."

Joanne doesn't look at him to say, "It was wonderful."

"You don't seem all that sad to be leaving."

"No, I'm not sad. I've seen it." She adds, softly, "It isn't for outsiders."

Neil settles into his seat-back. It was almost better when she was crying. He waits until he thinks of something good to say. "Joanne? It doesn't mean they're better."

"*I* know that." She watches more trees go by. She looks completely okay with things. "They wouldn't get Drumheller either."

"No. They damn well wouldn't."

It's a long ride but no one speaks. Neil feels hollow, and alone. He pictures Drumheller in a tourist brochure, then sees the inside of the dinosaur museum, and he knows what those giant trees reminded him of — they were like dinosaurs, the same thigh-bone thickness of dinosaur bones, only they were alive, and black in the fog, and he didn't like being in them. He thinks fondly, almost pleadingly, of his garage at home, its cement-cool in summer, and the old console TV he has in there for hot weather. For some reason he pictures a show last week when a beaten-up son squints up at a mean father and yells that he'll die a lonely death. Neil looks at Joanne over against her window and it only makes sense that he stay over here leaning against his. He's had enough crazy thoughts for a month and he wishes he could snooze, and then he must have because now he's being elbowed awake by Joanne who says, "Vicky and I are thinking Vancouver. The driver needs to know." Neal sees they're not even in the outskirts of Victoria, the meter reads $111 and is flying up fast. He's still working out how to charge all this to EdenTides Resort.

"Your call, honey. Your vacation."

"Yes!" whispers Vicky, clapping the tips of her fingers together. Somehow Vicky already knows where to go in Vancouver and apparently Joanne has promised her money for shopping. Neil finds it hard to look at his daughter. Out all night and he let her off the hook. When he does look at his girl he gets a feeling that, as of now, she's gone for good.

Joanne, nodding her head with each destination, says, "Hotel down*town*, we do *restaurants*, we do the *casino*."

"Your money," says Neil, steadily.

He's wondering what it will be like back in Drumheller, with his wife, who will now not be working, and whom he no longer knows. He pictures her finishing up the dishes and turning to him with expectations. She hates riding on the back of his Harley. He doesn't like to bowl. It will still be morning, clear and sunny out, all day long.

"*You* don't seem that okay." Joanne is staring at him in a way that tells him she's been doing it a while.

"I'm okay." He thinks, lonely death in the sun.

"I wish — I wish you'd had a good walk."

"I did have a walk."

"I mean like my walk."

He can't look at her any more. He wants to be home, despite the feeling that Drumheller will be gone now too.

"What's this on your hand?" Joanne taps his wrist near the smudge of bright orange paint.

"Nothing." He hides his wrist against his stomach. He's no longer proud of what he did.

"No, what?"

"Was helping buddy out with a little maintenance." He lifts his wrist and turns it in the light. It's an oil-based enamel which will take days to wear off his skin. It'll take more than that to come off the rock. "I was being, I dunno, passing aggressive."

Joanne leaves it at this. She smiles at several gulls wheeling over a dark, house-sized pile of something smouldering.

While Neil was waiting for the taxi, he did have his little walk. He knew what he was searching for, even what colour the paint would be, because ten small boulders lining EdenTide's driveway were freshly painted with it, a bright, ugly orange. The lock to the maintenance shack was a Schlage, which wasn't coming off, so he pried the latch screws. There was a half-can left, and a clean acrylic brush, medium-stiff, just right for the job. He also took a wire brush for scouring off any broken shell and for cleaning the rock down to base.

The sun had dried the square of rock face nicely. He did a neat job, but with all the alertly strolling ladies around he knew that news would get back to Andrew sooner rather than later so he kept it quick. In the four-foot square he painted a glossy orange M-U-S-C-L-E-S. He wasn't positive that's how you spelled it but he really didn't care much one way or the other.

THE WALK

Andy stood in his rented room. September again. The heavy familiarity of this childish purple bedspread, that smell of talc in the hall. He had been back mere minutes and already regretted it. He'd barely unpacked before old Mrs. Barastall invited him downstairs to be with her real family and watch her die. Why hadn't he just found an apartment this year, like everyone else? Even residence might have been better than this, especially now, with her dying right below.

Andy had no experience with death. When her son, Roger, the landlord, gave him her invitation, explaining about her being home from the hospital to die, the first thing Andy thought of was her chicken roll-ups. Old Mrs. Barastall cooked Sunday nights, the only meal Andy looked forward to here, and chicken roll-ups were his favourite. They took her all day to make, and she "made everyone pay for them" — Roger's little joke about the way his mother complained — by calling people to the table ten minutes before actually serving them. Then she'd appear with the dish and stand to ladle out the tooth-picked, dripping folds of breast meat and always say, "These take so much darned time to do right, but they're worth it." From his seat to her left, Andy always agreed with her.

But now, up in his room, unpacking his books and ripping open a new six-pack of white socks, he felt guilty for thinking about chicken roll-ups before attaching any weight to her death.

Whenever he told friends he lived in a boarding house, their first response was to glance skyward at an angle, attempting to picture what one was. Their second response was to ask, Why?

He didn't know why. The first year, he'd been late getting to town for the start of term, didn't know any better and ended up answering the Barastalls' newspaper ad out of hasty inno-cence. Just because Sandra showed him the room he felt obliged to say he would rent it. It hadn't registered at the time that he'd be eating with the family and watching TV with them and the old grandmother and all the rest of it. At first there was another boarder, but then only Andy, because in his second year they stopped renting the other room and moved old Mrs. Barastall down to it, telling her they didn't want her "tackling the stairs" any more. Andy suspected another reason: as he helped them move her dresser downstairs, he saw Roger's wink and Sandra's little bottomslap that followed mention of the newly empty room beside them. Now they could make noise.

"I'm just an old boarder now," Mrs. Barastall said, not smil-ing. Everyone including Andy laughed politely, assuming, hoping, it was a joke. It was her moving day, and she wore a grey track suit.

"You still own the place, Mom," Roger said back, smiling to tell her his was something of a joke too.

"Doesn't mean a thing," the old lady replied. She was good for that expression at least once a day, and what exactly she meant by it was no clearer now than usual.

That original ad had said, "Room for rent in character house," and though he knew what that meant he had fun for a while trying to think of the Barastalls as characters, though they were all fairly ordinary in most ways. As far as the house itself went, "character" was just a hopeful word for old.

Only gradually did Andy learn that boarding houses were archaic. In his second year, a potential girlfriend asked him if he lived there because he missed his family. He told her no, not bothering to fill her in on the detail of having only a mother he'd not seen since he was nine. She asked why else anyone would live at a boarding house. Andy didn't know what to tell her. He said, "Meals. I hate to cook." But it wasn't that. He didn't care for Sandra's cooking much at all.

Each year, with something like surprise he found he'd ended up here again. Here again eating Sandra's runny casseroles (and waiting for Sundays, and wishing Mrs. Barastall would cook more often). Here again listening to Sandra bicker with Roger, a navy man who filled the house with his presence during the weeks-long stretches he was home. And listening to Roger Junior, eleven, bounce an eternity of balls and taunt his older sister, May. Roger and Sandra also fought with May, who in Andy's first year was fourteen and shy and looked younger than she was. But she bloomed rapidly, and the family brawls really started "that night" — as they referred to it still — a couple of years ago when she came home with beer on her breath. Sandra's subsequent search through May's purse uncovered not only a condom but a ceramic moon amulet on the back of which was engraved, Coven of the West Kind.

From the yelling it was hard for Andy to tell what enraged Roger and Sandra more, the condom or the amulet. It didn't help any when old Mrs. Barastall, who had been listening too, entered to interrupt and say that witches weren't so bad, not at all, in fact. She'd known some in her time and — Roger's hissed "Mother! Leave!" put an end to her story.

Maybe the worst part about the boarding house was having to sit beside old Mrs. Barastall, in front of the TV, with nothing to say. (He sometimes thought he could smell her: under the waft of floral façade an undertone of sour.) Andy joked to himself that Mrs. Barastall was the main reason he struggled in school, and it was true that he did watch lots of TV with her, more TV than he normally would have. He just found it hard to walk by — harder than her own family did, in any case — without sitting down and watching a show with her. In his opinion she was too often left alone, especially after her cancer was diagnosed.

Friends would still ask how he could stand living "with, you know, other people around." They seemed to love being away from their families, and spoke with dread, only half joking, about a coming Christmas. Andy knew now that boarding houses were weird. He didn't know why he stayed. He didn't really like it, but he didn't really hate it.

He walked down the creaking back staircase to Mrs. Barastall's bedroom. "She says she wants to know how your summer went," was what Roger had said when inviting him down, his look suggesting his mother shouldn't be believed. Roger was only forty or so, yet Andy could not feel friendly toward him.

Roger was always stiff and severe, even with him, the other man of the house. Andy wondered if maybe it had to do with Roger being in the military, that he was somehow always on guard, always ready for war with other men. He reminded Andy of off-duty policemen he'd met.

He stood quietly at Mrs. Barastall's door, a hollow wooden one identical to his own. He heard voices, and then silence as a reedy whisper asked what sounded like a question.

Oh, he dreaded this. No so much Mrs. Barastall herself, whom he got on with well enough. Early on they'd developed a kind of rapport where it was tacitly agreed to say nothing controversial, thereby guaranteeing a comfortable sit at the TV. One should have a pleasant relationship with boarders, seemed her credo. Though she would break her own rule by sending him a sly glance after a risqué TV joke. He sometimes wondered whether he knew this old woman at all. Once, after a silent hour of watching two bad sitcoms in a row, she sighed and tilted her head in such a way that their age difference vanished, and said, "I wonder if there's nothing better for us to do than watch this crap."

No, what Andy dreaded was entering into family intimacy. Family was where Mrs. Barastall tried to toss her weight around. But no one listened to her. That's what made the arguments worse. That's what started them, in fact: she got nowhere and grew frustrated. It was her frustration Andy hated. Her frustration made him hate the whole family.

He saw the process as clear as day. Mrs. Barastall would say something reasonable enough, something starting with "In my time" or "Not that you asked my opinion but." No one would pay much attention. Roger might raise his eyebrows but keep on reading. Mrs. Barastall's next statement would come out harsher, quicker. Then a fight would start, Mrs. Barastall would make less sense and condemn "this poisonous age" and refuse to listen to them now, and the room would fall to a feuding silence.

And while Andy stayed clear of these feuds, he couldn't help but notice, for instance, that when Roger was gone Mrs. Barastall complained to Sandra about the setting of the thermostat, or the salt in the gravy. Because Mrs. Barastall was on a salt-free diet, Andy knew Sandra saw this particular complaint, tossed off with almost amiable chattiness, to be a huge accusation indeed. Andy actually thought it might be a macabre joke on the old lady's part, one that stung Sandra before she had a chance of getting it. Sometimes Andy thought that no one in the family knew old Mrs. Barastall very well at all. Not that the old lady helped much.

In any case it was clear a family war was being fought, a war of grotesque subtlety, but nonetheless a war, and Andy didn't like his role as foreign observer. They behaved a little better when he was around, but he could still hear the muffled explosions, feel the concussion in his gut.

Only ten minutes after arriving today he'd heard Roger and Sandra in the hall, Sandra crying.

"She . . . she accused me of withholding her pain pills. I couldn't believe she . . . how can she even think . . . ?"

"What did she actually say?" Roger asked.

"You know how she says things without really . . . I mean, I came with her pill and I wasn't more than ten minutes late with it and she looked at me and said, 'Do you think I don't need those any more?' What did she mean? I just can't stand . . ."

Roger told her it was going to be difficult, that his mother was afraid. Then he said curtly that Sandra wouldn't have to put up with it for long, which of course meant to say that his mother would die soon. The way he said it reminded Andy of the double-edged comments the old lady herself was so good at.

Andy eased Mrs. Barastall's door open and stepped quietly in.

Everyone was here. Roger sat on the bed edge, holding Mrs Barastall's hand, talking softly, something about sand peculiar to the Iraqi desert. Sandra sat in a chair smiling habitually, staring into the middle distance. May sat on the floor against the bed and looked up when Andy entered. She said "Hi" like a contemporary, like a friend, like a potential lover, in fact, and then quickly looked down. Andy realized she'd be eighteen now.

In the corner, barely able to sit still, sat Roger Junior. He squeezed a tennis ball, alternating hand to hand, to build up his wrist strength. Andy didn't like the kid much. Roger Junior was one of those kids who didn't have any friends and was a constant whiner, and you couldn't tell which of those was the chicken or the egg. And he seemed to have pinned all his hopes on sports. Now he looked scared to death, his eyes flicking to everything in the room except his grandmother. Mrs. Barastall had made a painful turn to watch him, and her eyes were knowing and gentle.

"Andrew, good," Mrs. Barastall said, noticing him now.

Her curly hair had receded dramatically and her shiny skull looked like an egg in a grey nest. Her eyes alone looked alive. They seemed to bear all the weight of a life that had got heavy, much heavier than her frail body. Every movement, every thought even, looked wrested up from within through intense effort. The eyes bulged. Perhaps the flesh around them had ebbed.

She was smiling at him.

"Look," she whispered. She flicked a finger at the new TV that sat on the dresser top behind him.

"Some night?" she whispered.

"Sure," said Andy. "*Friends* is on tomorrow night."

He almost added, in case she'd forgotten, *Friends* is on *every* night, the punchline to their joke, but didn't. He sensed the code of her dying, and it said you could be humorous but not frivolous. Perhaps unless you were family. Families forgave all.

"Did you know I have a stomach cancer?" Mrs. Barastall asked, her voice breaking out of the whisper into a sudden deepness, like a teenage boy's.

"Yes. I'm sorry."

"Me too, Andrew," she whispered, and the corners of her mouth lifted. She looked at him in the way that dissolved their ages again.

The Barastalls and Andy sat and talked. Nothing important was said. It seemed Roger tried to steer topics as far away as possible from the reason they were gathered. He tried to get his mother interested in Iraq again.

Andy grew impatient. Something here was crucial, and he felt a sense of waste. They should be summing up her life. Someone should be asking huge things of Mrs Barastall. He wasn't sure what. Perhaps: What's it like? Are there periods of peace? What do you think is going to happen when you die? It wasn't his place to ask anything like this. It occurred to him that he might be thinking these things only because he wasn't related. He didn't know what it was like to be related. They all looked clenched with hard, unspoken feeling.

A sudden breeze lifted the drapes, and everyone save Mrs. Barastall turned to the sight. Sandra said, "Hmm, windy." May agreed. Because of the drapes Andy noticed the pictures beside them on the wall, pictures of a woman he assumed was Mrs. Barastall. In several, looking twenty or so, she wore sporty white skirts and accepted tennis trophies. Another showed her on a beach surrounded by black men and women, some of whom had tattooed and scarred faces.

One significant thing was said when Mrs. Barastall asked May if she would please promise to finish a college degree. May promised, looking embarrassed, as if she had just taken part in something out of a corny movie. At the same time she looked stricken by the knowledge that she had just made a promise she would not easily break. She sucked a tendril of hair — Andy liked her long bronze hair — and stared at something past her feet.

"Can I shoot baskets now?" Roger Junior whined in a whisper to his father.

He was told "in a while."

"C'mon! You said ten minutes and I —"

Roger had his son hard by the arm and glared down a warning. The boy wouldn't look at him and began to struggle against his father's hold.

"You said!" Roger Junior looked wildly helpless, and ready to scream and thrash.

"Roggie!" Sandra pleaded.

Then a reedy, "Please . . . I'd like . . . to go for a walk."

So attuned was everyone to the possibility of Mrs. Barastall's whispered voice that it instantly stopped the commotion. Roger released his son's arm.

"Mother, you're too weak." He paused. "Why not . . . why not wait till you gain some strength?"

His mother gave him a look of disdain. Andy expected a fight now. Mrs. Barastall hated being lied to.

But she smiled.

"I'm eighty-two, Roger. And I would like to go for a walk."

Her eyes had a glow, and self-surprise in them. They drifted ceiling-ward, as if picturing something.

"I'll just go get the wheelchair," said Sandra, smiling rigidly and getting up.

"No, dear," whispered Mrs. Barastall. "I want to go for a walk."

Roger and Sandra met eyes. Roger raised his brows and held them. Sandra sent him the tiniest shrug.

"Maybe we could open a window, Elena?" Sandra asked.

"Walk," the old woman said, and shook her head.

"Maybe after a little nap, Mom," offered Roger, though he watched only his wife while saying it. Sandra was nodding hopefully.

"I would just like to go for a walk," Mrs. Barastall repeated. She looked close to tears now, or a fight had she the strength.

To his dismay, she looked at Andy. Painful as it was to meet her gaze, it would have been awful to look away. He knew exactly what she was trying to say to them. Horribly, no one else in her family seemed to.

"But Mom, I . . . don't think you *can* walk," Roger told her softly. He looked ready to cry as well. He clearly did not like saying such words.

"But I . . ." Mrs. Barastall began. A tear rolled onto her cheek.

"We can all . . . I mean, we can all help," Andy said. "One on each arm."

Roger and Sandra looked at each other again. Roger released a long sigh through his nose.

"Would you like your pill first, Elena?" Sandra asked her. "I know it's a bit early, but . . ."

"No, dear. As I've told you, I don't think I need them any more." She tried a smile. "I want to . . . enjoy this."

"But, Mom," Roger stepped in even as Sandra was pulling the blankets aside, "you can hardly even turn over as it is. A pill . . ."

"It's okay," Sandra said in instructive singsong, not looking at her husband as she helped Mrs. Barastall sit up, it seems having finally understood what Andy already knew, and what the old woman hadn't been able to say, which was that she wanted to walk one last time.

It took a long while and some organized patience to get her into slacks and a sweater. She wouldn't hear of wearing a bathrobe. Then socks and shoes. Absurdly, running shoes.

Roger Junior looked about to explode from fidgeting, but the hurt of his father's hand had scared him into keeping still.

They lifted her to standing and, at last, taking two- or three-inch steps, each one begun with a grimace and followed by a sigh, with a son at one armpit and a daughter-in-law at the other, Mrs. Barastall passed beyond her bedroom door.

She stopped, turned and whispered something in Roger's ear. Roger turned and said to his son, in a voice that broke, "Grammie says she hopes you will bounce a basketball as you walk with us."

They moved slowly down the sidewalk, so slowly that if watched from a distance they would have appeared not to be moving at all. Mrs. Barastall's foot lifted, moved a bit forward, descended carefully, touched down, and tested itself to bear weight. After a pause and several measured breaths, the other foot would begin the process.

During one such pause, Andy thought he heard her whisper, "To fly on one's feet." Then he wondered if instead she'd said, "To die on one's feet."

Mrs. Barastall often stopped altogether. Then she would pick up her head to see where in the neighbourhood she now stood. A particular house or tree would impart something to her and she would smile.

"Mrs. Gilroy has done well this year," she said almost a block from the boarding house, having noticed a healthy stand of late-blooming flowers. Then she directed her family's attention to the bright green window trim of the next house. "Eccentric," she whispered.

With her they walked, in a tight pack, a son at one side and a daughter by marriage at the other, then a grandson and granddaughter, and a boarder at the house she owned. It somehow seemed to Andy that she owned the neighbourhood too. That because of her age, and her patience, and the way her eyes knew the hidden details of the place, she owned it in a way that went beyond property and such. Even the way the sun lit her up spoke of this. It was easy to picture her as a girl here, a girl enjoying decades of the same sun on her face, its deep evening light angling in between these same houses.

Mrs. Barastall paused at an overhanging branch. A single leaf at the very end of the branch had already changed colour, orange with one corner dead brown. She brought her hand up and swatted it. It fell.

"That one's me," she said, and smiled to let them know she was joking.

They continued to move with her. The pace had bothered everyone at first, but now they were accepting. Even Roger Junior's basketball bounced in a steady, almost contented rhythm. The old woman's complete lack of hurry, her perfect patience, made Andy think of the word *royal*. Watching her, he also thought of the word *matriarch*, and for the first time felt he understood it.

Mrs. Barastall turned right then and caught Andy studying her. She smiled, her eyes very alive.

Andy didn't know why but, as soon as she resumed walking, he envisioned another culture, a society that revered old people. He pictured a strange parade, in which Mrs. Barastall was carried high up on a bannered platform, on the backs of bare-chested men about the age and uniform size of her son. Strangely, the images came less from any TV show or suchlike that he could remember, but more from the Barastalls themselves, including himself, walking along in this full evening light. He pictured people of all ages lining the path as she passed before them, she the longest-lived of all. They were comforted at seeing her, at seeing, in her, their own potential good life. At the end of the walk there would be rituals, and a feast.

Mrs. Barastall stopped again, and Andy almost bumped her. She turned around to look at May, who had dropped a pace back to walk beside Andy. Her grandmother caught her eye and then pointed a finger to indicate a house they were approaching.

"Doris," she whispered to May. "Doris Honey. She was a white witch. Lovely . . . sense of humour. And very good to me."

Mrs. Barastall continued her walk. They followed her almost imperceptible lead. Maybe it was the heavy light, Andy thought, but a power, it looked like, radiated from her. It was clear in her face. Andy wondered if Roger was seeing it too, for her son had stopped talking and now just stared.

It was pride at having lived fully and long, and it was pride at being able to walk. And, in a deepness that must be the well of her heart, she could feel something new, and surprising: a pride at having lived at all.

And she was proud to have this family, and to walk with them in such a neighbourhood. It was only natural that she should be proud. This was as colourful, as rich, as any walk before it had been. It was rich because it carried her whole family, who were her adornments, and who wore all their fear and love on their faces. And because one was an eleven-year-old boy who thought little of this event, wanting only to branch off and play his games — which was only right. It was colourful because here was her daughter-in-law who had never liked her but who respected her well enough now, just in time. And here was her granddaughter who had been drunk and who was no longer a virgin, but who had such a future, and whom today Mrs. Barastall had seen giving Andrew the boarder a sideways look that smacked of inevitability. So young, so ancient, so rich.

And here was her son, holding her up, a part of her own flesh that would keep carrying her after her body was gone.

It was no effort whatsoever to pull all of this behind her in a procession and show it off to the world, because it was now so ripe, because it had become her body and because she found pride in all of it.

Mrs. Barastall was not at all surprised to see the way the sun began to shine, and come out of itself, at that moment. Or that so many friends and neighbours who had been looking from their windows were now out of their houses to line the streets, dozens and dozens of them, waving to her with delight and welcome. So many of them she had not seen in years. Some looked mischievous in seeing her, like they could hardly wait to speak.

THE GREEN HOUSE

W e were walking by the house the day it got painted. All we knew was the Ditchburns had moved. I was fourteen, my four friends roughly that. We watched the new owners walk in and out pointing at things, proud and nervous. These owners seemed newer and more nervous than most. Some relative or suchlike stood high up a ladder rolling bright green paint under the eaves, a sharp, aggressive green that said nothing of trees or grass but instead some bad chemical. We knew the painter was one of them because he traded shouts in the same language. She was heavy, absurdly kerchiefed, and far too farmlike to fit in with our moms, or this our neighbourhood. Her shouts sounded, as Bobby Kerry put it, "like a dog trying to bark in human."

Only later in court did I learn where they were from.

"Who'd want a house that shitty colour?" This was me talking. Someone said retards, someone said pimps. Out of sight,

we exploded in guttural coughs, Chinese screams, spew of anything foreign and stupid that came to mind. It sounded so
lunatic I doubt the woman had any inkling such noise was our
version of her. But so it began.

Every neighbourhood has a Green House. Sometimes it's red,
sometimes purple, sometimes mauve with canary yellow
around the windows. They're all the same. Even kids know a
Green House when they see one. Neighbours talk behind the
backs of Green House owners and avoid them. The clothes
they wear show they're from a Green House as well. They send
their kids to school in awful shirts. You imagine they're well-
meaning and friendly, probably overly so. If you ever went to
their door and asked for a cup of sugar, they'd bring the cup
promptly, two cups, smiling too much.

Nothing excuses a Green House. And if the neighbours —
who were our parents — felt right to groan and sneer at one in
front of us, that was enough reason for us kids to show the
Green House no mercy at all.

We started innocently. That spring we hardly noticed them, so
busy were we with school and baseball, and a new thing —
stunned excitement about girls. But we passed the Green
House each day after school. Someone would look up and say,
God-look-at-that-fucking-house, and we might shout in
tongues again or make up stories. How they were inside right
now eating mice and cabbage, or screwing through a hole in
the sheet, or sponging their armpits at a handpump they'd
installed in their living room. We called them the Gooks.

Sometimes both the Gooks would be out in their new yard
raking and pruning. They looked almost normal, in fact more

boring than normal, though oddness was there if you looked
for it, which we did. She had the dumbness and square body of
a peasant in *National Geographic*. He was too thin and moved
too quickly with his shears. Hair black and full, a bushy moustache, and yet a very wrinkled face. I guessed he'd been sick,
though I didn't say so. His clothes suited neither these suburbs
nor an office. I could think of no other word to describe his
clothes than "communist."

With his shears and fast loamy hands, Mr. Gook was the
gardener, while Mrs. Gook, with her apt body, her hoes and
baskets, was the labourer. And as the spring climbed to
summer their garden became a remarkable thing. Flowers,
roses, blooms of all colours grew against each wall of the house
and out into the yard. These blooms were not only a childish
and gaudy ramble, it all clashed against the chemical green.

My parents had been calling them "the immigrants," and
now they took to calling their house "that toy box."

Walking to the park one evening (to sample some Valium
from the Kerry's medicine chest), we witnessed the Gooks
hosting a barbecue party in their front yard. None of us had
ever seen a barbecue in a front yard, exposed like that to the
street. Passing not twenty feet from what looked like huge
sausage sizzling on a brand-new grill, we were so embarrassed
at this show of uncool we had to put our heads down. But
worse was the party itself. We'd been raised on a version of
barbecue where same-looking couples, summer dressed, held
drinks and chatted. Sometimes kids were included, maybe a
few captive teenagers like us. The host might wear the latest
funny apron. The women's drinks would be light-coloured
and tinkle with ice; the men's darker in the glass, or a bottle of

beer. The host would shout, all would gather to eat, and that would be that.

The Gooks' party was an assortment of freaks, wonderful eye-food. Men in greasy T-shirts, big straight-haired silent women wearing starched bags. An old man in a wheelchair, smoking a massive curling pipe. Two fat old ladies — we couldn't believe this bounteous fuel for scorn-out — dressed head to toe in black, sitting away from the rest and not speaking. The few kids our age, one of whom waved to us but got nothing back, seemed of another world as well, their haircuts and clothes reminding us of a corny Ol' Yeller pack of hicks. The one who waved wore a jean jacket proclaiming Sgt. Pepper on the back, but without the jeans and sneakers required of it his hickness was all the more glaring. All the guests guzzled from great wicker jugs of red wine, or from a bottle of clear booze that looked homemade too. A man my dad's age was weeping openly and thrashing his arms around. Others tried to calm him but ended up thrashing their arms too. All this in a front yard.

Hours later, when too much lethargy pushed us from the park, we happened upon a dead squirrel. Dave MacIver toed it onto its back and said, "*I* know." We got excited again for a few minutes, though no one moved very quickly. The plan was to put it on the Gooks' barbecue. We carried it with a forked stick and stood at the Gooks' gate. All was dark and quiet.

"But they might think it just fell dead of the roof," I said, always the thinker.

Al Cody snuck between two houses and came back with a toy boat, a bulbous red plastic tug with a smiling face comprising the deck and smokestack.

"Still not enough," Bobby Kerry said, digging in his pocket. Out came a dollar bill. A sacrifice at our age, but the perfect touch.

We crept down the walk to the Green House and then quickly back, stifling giggles. A squirrel, a happy-boat, and a dollar bill sat on the grill, waiting for the Gooks in the morning.

We weren't bad kids. Except for Dave McIver we were decent students, and athletic to boot. But though it's true that for a time our actions were fouled by the darker humours of adolescence, I did and still do blame Dave MacIver for much of what happened that Green House summer. He'd failed a grade or two and was older than us. At fifteen MacIver looked like a mature pug. His head was too large, his nose too small. A front tooth stayed chipped for years. It did occur to me that, of us friends, his family most resembled the Gooks — they were the poorest in Deep Cove, his parents had accents, his father shouted and drank, and their small house stayed unpainted for as long as Dave's tooth stayed chipped — but I never put two and two together. Why we put up with him and even followed his lead I'm not sure. Likely because he was bigger and tougher, glamour for fourteen-year-old boys being identical to glamour for animals.

All the same, I didn't talk to Dave MacIver much after the summer. And when it came to naming names, his jumped off my tongue easily and without any guilt at all.

The week after our barbecue joke, the Gooks had that haunted look. Bobby Kerry, who'd just seen a movie, said they looked like Italians who got a dead fish in the mail. MacIver didn't get Bobby's joke and just butted in and hissed out his latest plan. Yes, we'd all noticed those wine jugs in their carport.

We began by making leisurely crank calls on weekend nights to see if they were out. It was the usual embarrassingly bad kid stuff: Hello, is your refrigerator running? etc. Al Cody put on a passable German accent and deep voice, pretending to be a government official who wanted to see their papers. When I took my turn I heard a raspy female voice say, "Vot?" and then a babble at someone away from the receiver. Clearly, they hadn't been understanding one silly word. Only MacIver took a different tack. Tense at the phone, his lips pulled back from his teeth, he'd yell at the top of his voice, "*Fuck off faggot freaks.*"

The next Saturday night they didn't answer so we wandered over. There in the empty carport sat the jugs, five of them, all in a neat squat row. We looked around, hopped the fence, and hustled in. One of the jugs had a thermometer thing, lively with bubbles, stuck in its top. This MacIver plucked and broke casually under his foot. For the first time I had inklings. The look on his face scared me.

We ignored the fizzing jug and those of us who could manage it took turns pissing into a nearly empty one. We lugged the other three out and over to the park, two of us leading and trailing as lookouts. Bobby Kerry dropped and broke one. I suspected even then that he did it on purpose, for he'd been the most squeamish about this prank, and when we sat to drink the wine he had a candy-ass excuse for heading home.

But drink it we did. Most of it, in fact, between five of us, until later when three older guys shouldered in and hogged the rest. We sat around like calm professional drinkers and bragged about the deed, and as we got into it we took turns trying to come up with the face that best showed the Gooks tasting our piss, which had us falling off our logs and almost pissing ourselves. In a quieter moment I found myself remembering what I'd seen through the Gooks' kitchen window while we were in the carport. I wasn't sure what had struck me about the inside of the house. Lit by the streetlight, the pots and pans were somehow a little different. It all looked very clean. The one odd thing was a picture I could barely make out on the dining-room wall. It was of a giant human hand, very lifelike with the wrinkles and nails and the rest, but shooting out of the hand were these wonderful curling flames, some pink, others green. It was like a photograph but with great special effects. Otherwise there was an odd calm to the house, a stillness I found very likeable. Maybe it was what all empty houses had, I didn't know. Maybe it was my thief's adrenalin. But the peculiar stillness of that house felt welcoming. It made me like the Gooks. Naturally I said nothing about this to my friends, either in the carport or at the drunken bonfire. They, and especially MacIver, didn't go in for details.

The wine hit us hard. We were soon screaming and laughing, and before too long puking. I twisted an ankle badly, and the next morning had no idea how. All of us felt hellish for a day. Except for MacIver it was our first major hangover. And in that ragged, godless, nauseated state we found ourselves blaming the Gooks and saying things like, Stupid house. Shit wine. Dumb bastards.

School was over now. Trying out an old skateboard, I was coasting empty-headed down the slight slope toward the Green House, and could see Mr. Gook sitting in his front yard in a chair. My feelings about them had levelled off: it wasn't their wine but our own gulpings that had made us sick; since seeing into their house I felt I knew them a little; in general I felt sorry for their foreignness enough to want to let them be. In fact I hadn't even taken part in MacIver's latest prank, though it was one of my favourites, the dog shit on the doorstep thing. The idea was to collect fresh doggy-do in a paper bag, lay it at their door, ring the bell, light the bag on fire and run. With any luck you get to see a guy stamp a fire out and get shit on his slippers in the process. In any case, I heard it didn't go well at the Gooks' — the top of the bag had burned away and gone out by the time Mr. Gook came to the door. He just stooped and looked into the bag, scanned the area for faces, then slammed the door.

Skateboard noise made Mr. Gook look my way as I rolled up. I saw he'd been scribbling notes onto a bunch of papers and charts on his lap. Again, the backyard would have been the place for this sort of thing. But what the hell, I thought, and waved to him. He was looking right at me after all, and I felt magnanimous. He answered with a lifting of a couple of fingers. Clearly a case of an adult dismissing a child.

This response made me angry. I don't know what I'd expected. Some kind of kowtowing. Something goofy or overly friendly. He was an immigrant and this was my neighbourhood. That he was allowed to live here because of my tolerance, my permission, was an absurd thought, but that was exactly how I felt, how we all felt.

He studied my skateboard as if he'd never seen one before. Then he looked up to my face again. He studied that too. His eyes were remarkable things, the kind of silver-blue colour that seems deep and empty and tries to pull you in. The eyes made the rest of his wrinkled face secondary. His gaze was matter-of-fact, one eyebrow up a little. You could tell he gazed at things like this, at anything I had to offer, a thousand times a day. My anger fell to embarrassment, for his eyes made clear that he was not only an adult but an adult way smarter than me.

Maybe they'd learned something because they held the next barbecue in the back. This part of the property was sur- rounded by a fence plus lots of bushes and trees, so we hardly had to hide as we watched them.

It was a smaller gathering. The old man with the weird pipe sat across from one of the black widows. There was one couple the Gooks' age (it was the weeping man, sober this time) and the kid with the jean jacket. He wore sneakers, but the same hick-brown pants. For the most part they sat around in chairs, sipped and talked in their dog-language. A whole chicken had been plopped spread-eagle on the grill. We knew there was no way they were going to get that chicken done without an elec- tric spit. Mrs. Gook got up from time to time to turn the bird, but it kept rolling back onto one of its flat spots.

In a minute we were bored, so Al Cody started things off, flicking a small pine cone into the yard. After a strategic delay one of us would toss another, each cone more daring, landing closer and closer. I flicked a high wild one that arced and hung deliciously. We ducked when it ticked off the old man's shoul- der. He turned and regarded some branches that weren't exactly overhead but close enough to satisfy him. Next MacIver tossed a deliberate shot that fell into the barbecue. We hunched and hissed, "Oh shit," while all heads turned to look. Some scanned the sky for passing birds. Mr. Gook was staring expressionless in our direction. But he didn't move, and soon they were talking again.

"Fuck it," Cody whispered. "Spray and run." We each gath- ered a handful of cones and climbed carefully to our haunches. We checked to see if everyone was ready. Cody signalled with a quick dip of head and then we were all grunting, throwing, and leaping away. I'd seen MacIver scoop up the rock and now I heard the *crack* off a head and looking back saw Mrs. Gook go down on one knee. "*Ass*hole," I hissed as I sprinted. If anyone chased, they were no match for young men who knew, like rats know sewers, the secret veins of their neighbourhood.

I never told anyone, but several times over the following weeks I went by the Green House at night to stare in their carport window while they were asleep. Streetlight got in just enough to show me that festive interior, and in particular the flaming hand picture on the far wall. I always got that good feeling. I thought of the word "haven." The Gooks had made themselves a haven here.

I avoided the Green House for a while after the coning, but I couldn't help passing it one day when Mr. Gook was out in his front yard. I meant to speed by, but couldn't resist watching him, bent and scribbling over his papers like that. Coming closer, I saw he marked a chart with coloured pencils. A photo album lay open on the lawn at his feet and he'd lean out to study it before marking his chart. What sort of work? Maybe he researched his relatives, his family tree. Squinting harder at the album I made out only abstract shapes and swirls of colour.

I'd slowed almost to a stop. Maybe it was the sight he made: under a perfect bright day, under a noble shade tree, this wise-looking man examined colourful things. We had just heard about the Greeks in school, and I had an image of Socrates teaching in a place like this.

I waved. He had to have seen it. And I said hi, not loud but loud enough. He made no sign. So I hurried on, embarrassed. How dare a Green House Gook be a snob. Ready to dismiss him as a dumb shit, I considered options. Deafness, for one. Or his scholarly concentration blinded him to all else. Or perhaps he suspected me to be one of the tormenting hoodlums, and was doing me a kindness by turning the other cheek. I chose this last one.

I went along with the break-in for two reasons and they were both good. I've thought a lot about it since and I still think they were good. The first reason was selfish — I wanted to check the house out more. The second was only good — I wanted to protect the house from Dave MacIver.

We were so nervous. Even in the planning of it we fell to whispers, and any jokes came out stuttered and fake. No one really wanted to do it, but we all had to sound like we did. That's not true — MacIver was eager.

We knew now that Sunday was their night out. We gathered at the backyard fence. Besides MacIver and me, only Al Cody and Bobby Kerry had shown up. We watched Mr. rev the car until Mrs. appeared bearing a casserole and basket of bread. Off they went. We hopped the fence and, since it was the height of summer, we had our pick of half-open windows. We chose the breakfast nook.

MacIver went in first so I made sure I followed. We'd agreed not to break or steal anything big enough to bring us real trouble, but one look at MacIver there in the kitchen told me to watch him closely. Hunched, breathing hard, and eyeing everything faster and faster as if he might now own it all, he seemed an animal in some grim paradise.

I admit to feeling a sort of euphoria myself. It was wonderful in there, so cool, so dim, the bright colours standing out sharply. I felt so full of oxygen I no longer had to breathe. Again, maybe this was the adrenalin of thieves in a dark new place. But I felt acquainted with this house. I felt like the house.

The last in, Bobby Kerry no sooner touched the floor than he panicked and yelled, "They're here!" He scrambled back out and was gone, leaving just us three.

Following MacIver through the dining room, I stopped under the flaming hand. Dramatic up close, it *was* a photograph of a hand, surrounded by a rosy mist, with green flames curling out the fingertips.

On the other wall was a blow-up of Disneyland, Mrs. Gook arm in arm with Scrooge McDuck, her smile girlish as could be, her wide-set eyes half-closed and teary. Under the picture a bookcase held mostly dictionaries — English-Polish, English-French, English-Russian, English-Hebrew — and two books had a special place: *Welcome to Canada* and *Canadian Fact Book*.

A fiercely whispered "Just *this*" made me turn to see MacIver take a knife in a jewelled scabbard off the mantel. More a sword than a knife, its curve made a quarter moon and reminded me of Oriental barbarians, who could slash with it, not stab. MacIver worked it into his belt and before I could say a thing he whirled at me and stiffened up tall and said, "It's my *birthday*." We both knew it wasn't his birthday. His eyes were crazy.

I turned away, a host who'd lost control, as MacIver sprayed two decks of cards, a violent shower of squares, around the room. This had Cody giggling like a girl. I decided I'd be the last one out and clean up as best I could. But I couldn't stand here and watch.

I found the door to the downstairs. Descending to one immense basement room, lit only by dusk through two window wells, I flicked the switch. I saw right away that while the upstairs was hers, this was his. The walls were grey gyprock. The floor was still cement. The greyness was overpowering. Two walls displayed group portraits, his family, I decided. Stepping closer, I saw bearded men and sour women, in severe unsmiling rows. All were black and white, but from the looks of their clothes and the landscape, colour film wouldn't have added much. A wedding picture of the two of them hung in a special place, it too a drab grey. They looked frightened.

A third wall displayed certificates and diplomas, most in foreign lettering but some not. The Indiana Center for Psychic Studies. The Parapsychology Institute of America. The Kirlian Institute Pioneer's Award. All to H. H. Karmapov.

The fourth wall was a giant black felt curtain, dense and light-proof. I pulled it aside to find another room, a developing room with trays and bottles of chemicals and, in the middle, resembling a drill-press, harnessed on poles to point down, what looked to be an odd black camera.

I felt like I'd walked into a rainbow. The walls were jammed with pictures of hands, feet, leaves, flowers, all emitting flames and swirls of violet, gold, lime and rose. One single fingertip, enlarged three feet square, revealed its whirlpool of fingerprint, from the centre of which issued a needle-thin ray of crimson.

I stared for I don't know how long before I noticed the books, neat stacks and rows of *The Kirlian Annual* and *Kirlian Photography*. A single hardbound book had his name on the spine, just *Karmapov*. I plucked it out and thumbed through and saw in its pages the same leaves, hands, and feet that hung on these walls. One appeared to be a corpse's hand, with nothing surrounding it but a kind of muddy mist. I found the dining-room picture in one of the full-page feature shots.

I ran up the stairs. Mr. Karmapov was famous. Even MacIver would be amazed by this stuff. But in the kitchen I stopped, hearing their noises upstairs. A thud, wild laughter. At the foot of the stairs a bottle of perfume lay open, dripping heavy sweetness into the air. I didn't dare show them the magical basement. I wanted them out of here entirely, out of Mr. Karmapov's house.

In the upstairs bedroom they'd pulled out drawers, it looked like MacIver had slashed into some pillows with his birthday knife, and Mr. Karmapov's ties were cut in half and scattered. They'd found condoms and blown one up and tied it. The bathroom, where they were now, was strewn with Q-tips and toilet paper, and MacIver was lipsticking the mirror.

"Jesus, we gotta go, we been here an hour," I lied, trying to sound scared. I turned away in a hurry, took some fake pounding steps downstairs, then tiptoed back up and ducked into a guest room. In a minute Cody and MacIver descended. I started in the bedroom as quietly as I could, stuffing and putting back drawers, gathering snipped ties. I didn't know what to do. Write him a note, apologizing? Pay him back in secret? I thought of running home for my dad's ties. But I just stuffed all the damage into a pillowcase, to take.

I went to work in the bathroom, scooping, stuffing. I winced as something smashed downstairs, then more laughter. On the mirror and part of the wall MacIver had left a perfect image of himself: misspelled obscenities and one large swastika. I started on the swastika, remembering the Hebrew dictionary.

Then from downstairs a muffled shout, some shuffling and banging. A car door closed, a kitchen door crashed.

"Vot? Vot?"

I don't know why I was running down to them, the Karmapovs, but running I was, down the stairs, glad the swastika was off at least, glad my pillowcase held most of the destruction. I may just have thought it, but I may in fact have yelled, "I've got it almost clean, it's almost clean."

I found them embracing in the kitchen, Mr. Karmapov crooning and stroking his wife's head. They swayed. It was as if they'd done this before. They swayed over the bright yellow of a broken mustard jar on the floor, and squirted ketchup, and a sneaker Al Cody had lost escaping out the window. Mr. Karmapov was staring across into the dining room at his flaming hand picture. It was smeared with molasses.

He turned to look at me now, and doing so he smiled, snorted, and shook his head. I was no big deal. His cold blue eyes bulged wide and seemed to be taking in far more than just me. Later, in the hearing, I learned he had eyed other thieves, and brutal police, and acts of cruelty I couldn't begin to imagine. Grimly smiling, he released his wife and whispered to her and she obediently went to the phone. Still smiling he moved to the middle of the kitchen and squared his shoulders, blocking my way to the door. He looked cruel, like he hoped I would try getting past.

I stood where I was. I could smell him. It was a smell of rage, and it was also a foreign smell. I said I was sorry, looked to both of them, and got a response from neither. Now, with another snort and a fresh smile, from his wife's basket on the counter Mr. Karmapov pulled a square, black box, a twin of the camera in the basement. He cranked a lever around and around and the camera whined and the harshest lime-green light issued from a little flashlight-thing on its top. He pointed the camera at me and the white-lime beam made it hard to look.

"You scared," Mr. Karmapov said, so softly he probably didn't care if I heard him. "You be very colour." He added, louder, "Smile."

THE GODS TAKE OFF THEIR SHIRTS

Another day's headache is almost gone. The taxi delivers me and there's Jay in his cluttered carport. He's standing calmly, he looks normal. I don't know what I expected. He's taking a puffy ski jacket from a dry cleaner's bag. He treats the filmy bag gingerly. I see it's the bag he wants and I'll bet he took that ski jacket in just so he could get one.

He hangs the clean jacket from a nail in the carport wall. Jay's is one of those trusting carports where people could come in and take stuff. Other nails hold rain gear, and what look to be some of Penny's dresses and windbreakers. Penny left Jay maybe five years ago now. As far as I know he's been alone in this house since then. Also in the carport are stacked paint cans, car tires, road-hockey sticks and such, plus some chairs that one day might get repaired. It's not the kind of stuff thieves would walk even the length of a driveway to grab, but middle-of-the-night teenagers could have themselves a time.

"What's wrong with your car?" is how Jay greets me.

"What do you mean?"

"The taxi."

I tell him I took a cab because I assume tonight involves beer.

"I'm not going to," he says, "but feel free."

He's wearing jeans and a T-shirt and so am I. For some reason this bothers me. I watch him smooth out his bag, and notice the candles and strips of balsa wood scattered on a table.

After waiting another moment I ask, "You have any? Beer?"

He thinks there might be a few cans in the fridge, at the back, I'll have to dig around. It's funny seeing old friends like Jay, because even though he's around forty, like you, your history is one of being young and crazy together, so you still see him, and by extension yourself, as young and crazy. Or maybe it's, seeing him, you're reminded you're not crazy any more but want to be, as though it's a good thing. For better or worse it's in the air, even though he called earlier today to tell me he has a brain tumour and wants to spend the evening together.

I return from rooting in the fridge, beer in hand, and there were only two others, I'll have to make a beer run somehow. Taking a perky first sip, I recognize now what Jay's laid out on the table: stuff to build a UFO candle-bag. I'm amazed I remember.

"Good," he says. "You found one."

"You're not drinking?"

"Actually," says Jay, "I'm fasting."

"Because of . . ."

Jay turns to me, eyes full of energy. His hair needs washing but he looks sturdy as can be.

"Yup," he says. For a moment I'm worried he isn't going to say any more. But he does. "I've been reading lots about it. It actually might help. Fasting burns your fat and your toxins first, and then it does tumours at about the same time it does muscles. Then it does organs — you don't want that, so you have to stay on top of it."

I tell him I didn't know any of this.

"It's one thing you can do. It's easier than one of those special diets." He gives me a half-smile. "Fasting you don't have to do anything at all."

I'm sweating, it's hot, my beer is already gone. It's the perfect situation for a cold can of beer and my middle has warmed up and spread with that first little bliss. It must be eight o'clock but it's the longest day of the year, the solstice, and feels like afternoon. On the phone Jay had mentioned the solstice and said the evening would be "exactly perfect for launching."

"So what do they say? The doctors."

"Not much. It's still early."

"Well, I mean, when did you find out? And . . . You know — what's going on with it?" It's hard to come out and ask, Are you going to die? Or, How much time?

"Well it's not exactly official yet. Not 'confirmed.' "

"I mean are they sure it's cancerous and all that?"

"Well, no, but it is."

I relax at this. Jay might not even have cancer. We can relax this evening and maybe I can get Jay to have a good time.

"So you don't really know."

"No. I know."

"How?"

Jay gives me another half-smile and raised eyebrows. "How do we know anything?"

He turns and glides the long, air-light bag over to the table as if it were a ghost. I tell him I'm amazed he's remembered. We'd tried this when we were perhaps fifteen.

"It'll work this time," he says. "I've got it figured out. I made this hoop thing."

He lifts his hoop, made of curved balsa wood the width and thickness of a toenail, formed to fit the big mouth at the bottom of the bag, maybe two feet in diameter. He tosses it up and catches it, showing me it is light yet strong, a hoola-hoop for faeries. He points to the white candles and tells me he timed one and they burn an inch a half-hour. So it's my job, he says, to cut eight one-inch candle stubs. A small fine-toothed saw lies beside the candles. It's a job he could've done himself in two minutes. So he's been thinking of ways to include me.

"I'll get on it," I tell him, flipping my can into a blue recy-cling box as I go inside for another. I haven't asked him why he's doing this silly UFO thing. Only when my hand is on the fridge handle do I see that this might be exactly what a guy with a brain tumor might do.

I return as Jay ties, with thread, two strips of balsa to the hoop so they cross at the middle. This cross will carry my candle stubs. Another job he gives me is to stick the stubs to the wood with a few drops of melted wax. My headache still flirts so I'm glad to be using my hands.

"It screwed up last time because remember we had only the one strip," Jay tells me. I have no recollection whatsoever. That night, so long ago, also probably involved beer. I do recall a few of us launching something that caught fire right away, the plas-tic shrivelling and burning instantly. I think I remember it burning with no sound.

"Great," I say, probably unconvincingly because Jay goes on to explain that the reason it burned last time is because the candles were too close to the bag, "and *boom*," he says. "This time we can huddle them all in the middle."

"Sounds good."

Jay does look like he's lost some weight, but I don't know if brain cancer is one that does that.

"I thought of this after hearing about the Japanese balloons in World War Two. You ever hear about those? That they launched at us?"

I hadn't.

"They launched thousands. Hot air balloons. Unmanned hot air balloons that carried sort of these gas firebombs. The plan was to have them hit all over the West Coast, start all these forest fires, and burn up all the western forests."

"Why?"

"They had altimeters and if it got too low it'd drop a sand-bag and gain altitude again. One man in Oregon was killed getting hit with a sandbag. He was the only casualty of the Second World War on the North American continent. Did you hear about the Japanese sub that shelled Vancouver Island, they think it was aiming at a lighthouse, but it missed?"

I tell him I don't know if I've ever heard any of this. "So are you going to be going in for more tests?" I ask him.

"MRI in two months."

"That's a — ?"

"Brain scan."

"That's a bit of a wait," I tell him. But if he has one scheduled at all, there must be something to this.

"Actually they wanted to do it next week. I got them to delay it, so I could fast."

"Ah . . . Why?"

"Have to give the fast time to work. Now it'll be gone, cured, vanished when they scan it. It'll look like nothing was ever there."

"That'd be *great*. But, you know, then you won't know if you ever even had something."

He doesn't look at me this time and softly says, "I have something."

I saw candles into one-inch stubs. Soon my shoes are covered with a wax dust, which looks like confectioner's sugar on two chocolate loaves. Jay tells me to shave a stub down a bit more and I do. I'm not sure why I don't believe in his tumour. Jay was always the first guy in our group to do *any*thing. He would laugh at this little funny but I don't want to try it on him unless I can slide it into the conversation, which now wanders paths of gossip about other old friends. But if anyone knew they had a tumour without really knowing, it would be Jay. He was the guy who knew things. He was the guy who had us all try this vitamin I can never remember the name of, that made you flush red in the face and everything went pins and needles, and Jay said if you didn't have that reaction it meant you had at least mild schizophrenia. He was first with everything. When we were sixteen he got hold of a bottle of absinthe and he described its properties and history while the rest of us passed it around and guzzled. He was the first one to get a car. He was also the first one to quit drinking for a while, and get a mountain bike, and eat healthy food, and experiment with getting in shape. In the last ten years or so I haven't seen him much and you hear rumours about this and that, but I can sum up Jay for myself by remembering him as the guy who, while the rest of us stumbled along a snowy trail in the dark, halfway up Cypress Mountain, looking for Rooney's cabin, Jay stopped with genuine excitement and pointed to the stars on the horizon and wouldn't let us go until we all saw the rare comet. It was hardly visible he said, and I only pretended to see it, but the main point is that Jay knows a lot about a lot of things, and I have to say I've never known him to be wrong. Maybe even about a guy getting killed by a Japanese sandbag in Oregon.

"Try tipping it upside down," Jay tells me.

I turn the hoop-cross over and only one candle stub falls from the balsa wood. We light a candle and drip a few more drips and get it stuck on properly.

"Remember Rooney's cabin?" I ask.

"I remember your puke hole in the snow."

"Fine."

"How's Pam doing?" he asks, casually as can be.

"Long gone," is all I say.

"Sort of heard that. Divorce too, right?"

"Totally." I think, enough of this.

"You with anyone else?"

"Not to my knowledge."

"Not tossin' the dogwater to anyone in particular?"

I have to smile, "toss the dogwater" being Rooney's term for sex, something we haven't heard in more than twenty years. Decent memory, Jay, for a brain tumour.

Jay carefully fits the bag opening around the hoop, a tube of Crazy Glue at the ready. Crazy Glue scares me. The stories of eyelids glued shut and needing surgery, practical jokes involving faces stuck to frying pans and such.

"Imagine having no eyelids," I offer.

"You'd want to be back in before sunrise."

"You would."

"So you're not with anybody," Jay persists.

"Nope."

"Nobody on the horizon?"

"Not even over the horizon."

"You still looking?"

"Is this, like, a talk show?"

I think I meant "encounter group," but you go with what comes out. I'm reminded that Jay can get pushy. I wonder again about brain tumours and decide I will only be nice. Plus the three beers are done and I'm going to ask him to please ask a neighbour for some. I hate using taxis for booze runs and in any case I'm not sure I have the cash.

"I'm just wondering if you're unencumbered," he says. "I have sort of a proposition."

Who knows where this is going — I'm a little nervous now. Jay is minutely dabbing glue to the outside of the hoop and pressing plastic bag hard to the wet spot. He looks practised at it.

"Well, so the thing is, why I called, and what I'm looking for —"

"First? Jay? I could really use another beer. This is sort of my night out." I'm using any leverage I have, considering I might soon be losing it. "I was wondering if maybe you have a neighbour who's a buddy and might have a spare something lying around? That I could replace?"

Jay looks at me thoughtfully. I'm thinking one pupil is a little larger than it should be. He looks a bit like David Bowie, and I don't think he used to.

Jay drops his gaze and appears to appraise his feet.

"Seeing as it's your night out, I think I can find something. Georgio over there makes his own and has a million bottles stashed downstairs." The half smile. "He's actually glad when someone likes it. Keeps your glass topped up."

Jay settles the bag and hoop onto the table in an orderly pile and heads down his drive. He asks back over his shoulder, "Red okay?"

"See if you can get two or three," I tell him, not too ashamed of myself, watching him cross the street and then the neighbour's lawn. He walks like he's always walked. Who knows.

I don't know what I thought Jay's proposition might be, but it's weird enough.

"I'm looking for a housemate," is what he says. "Maybe a helper."

"A helper."

"If this fast doesn't work. If nothing works. If it gets bad and I can't do certain stuff." The smile again. "Might need some help."

Jay's finished gluing the bag to the hoop and I'm settling in with some wine, which I believe is very good Italian, though I may just think that because I know the maker's name is Georgio. But it's rich and robust for homemade. It's Jay's fault that I'm drinking it from the bottle. When he lugged the four bottles up the drive (Georgio in his front door waving to me from across the street), he asked if I wanted a glass or just wanted to drink it straight from the bottle, taunting me for what he takes to be my desperation. So I called him on it and said no glass was required. Then I one-upped him and grabbed a screwdriver, hammered it with a chunk of firewood, drove the cork down, took a good slug, wiped my mouth on my wrist, and pronounced the wine "acceptable." I can get contrary when people accuse me of drinking too much. I'll use a corkscrew and wineglass for the next bottle.

"Don't they have people for that? 'Helping professionals?'" I ask him.

"Christ, who has the money?"

"I guess they're pricey."

"You wouldn't believe it."

It looks like our UFO is ready when Jay glues shut the little hole at the top of the bag where the hanger-hook goes through. What we have is an inflatable bag about five feet tall and three wide, at the bottom of which is a light frame holding eight candles, which will be lit, and fill the bag with hot air, and cause it to float, up, up over the neighbourhood, which will be able to see only a cluster of unidentifiable lights moving in the sky. That's the theory, anyway, our only other UFO having burned, twenty-five years ago, before it left the ground. I notice how tricky it's going to be to get the candles lit.

"We should put this pooch in the air," I suggest.

"Let's give it fifteen minutes." Jay stands, hands on hips, gazing into the evening sky. It's just past sunset. "I want it to be exactly right. When it's sort of a darker purple." He nods toward the horizon.

"How do we get these candles lit?"

Jay explains that the vacuum cleaner there in the corner will blow the initial hot air into the bag, filling it, keeping it away from the candles, which will then be lit "with teamwork and surgical co-operation."

He asks me what I think. About what, I say. He says that part of the deal would be me getting free room and board because of the eventual "helping" part.

"What if you don't get sick and no helping takes place?"

"We'll have to see how that goes. Even by the end of this fast, I'll need someone to cut the grass and stuff. Anything heavy. Plump my pillow."

"You've thought this out."

"Have to."

"So I guess you're asking me to move in."

"That's why I wanted to know if you're with anybody."

"When do I have to let you know by?"

"Soon as possible. I need to find somebody. I just thought of you yesterday and called."

I decide not to be stung by this. I ask, "Who knows if we'll start slapping each other over what kind of Campbell's soup to have every night." Jay's checking his fingers for glue, nodding. I add, "I mean, we haven't hung out for a while."

He points his chin at his house. "It's bigger than it looks. We can pretty much avoid each other if we want." He looks to a corner of the carport. "There's a TV in that box. It's only twenty inches but we could each have our own TV."

"So why me?"

Jay meets my eye soberly. Maybe I want some sort of declaration about friendship, about the magic trust of knowing a person since kindergarten.

"I dunno. I guess because you can."

"Because I can."

"Because you're free. Wife. House. Kids. I went down a list of people." He smiles, but sadly. "There's hardly anyone as free as you, man."

I wonder how much Jay knows. What the gossip is. Why I left that last job. Why I no longer drive a car. How what might look like self-destruction has been a case, a long case, of bad luck. I firmly believe that depression is bad luck. Who it hits and who it doesn't hit and how long it stays — who has control over that? Does he know how I tortured and then killed a beautiful life with Pam?

"And I really have to ask you one thing," Jay says. "Can I get personal?"

I shrug as if to say "obviously," though we never have gotten personal, unless we did one day in kindergarten.

"No judgement, okay? But I have to ask you straight out." He raises his eyebrows at the bottle I've just put on the table, dented cork resting in the quarter-inch of wine that's left.

"Okay."

"So, I have to know, is every night your 'night out'? I mean I have to know, if you're helping me. I have to know if you'll be reliable."

"It's a fair question." And it's one I'm not sure how to answer, seeing as the truth is the only answer possible, and seeing as every night for the past while has indeed been a sort of night out.

"Don't mean to pry, but obviously it's something a guy — a fifty-pound bald guy — will need to know." He smiles and I smile back, grateful he's turned it into a joke, which he continues. "You know, like if the garbage is never going to be taken out and it's going to be Led Zeppelin at two in the morning."

"It'll be the Rolling Stones."

"That's a little better."

"But four in the morning."

We're both smiling pretty good though Jay's eyes are still focused on a spot in space exactly between us and he's waiting for my answer. I wonder if he knows he's giving me an opportunity. Then I wonder if it was part of his plan.

"I'd be reliable," I tell him, making myself meet his eye.

He nods. "I sort of knew that."

But I tell him I need to chew on it and I'll let him know before I leave tonight.

"Well, *if* you leave," he jokes back.

Not long after sunset, I'm sipping superb Italian from a crystal glass. Jay uses the vacuum's ass to fill the bag and we gently guide it, half-floating, into the backyard. Both armed with a

long, decorative fireplace match we light the candle stubs and
it's indeed a surgical procedure to get all eight lit without
touching flame to plastic film and ending it in an instant. In
this windless dusk, as the bag rises slowly from Jay's weedy
backyard, and moves even more slowly, almost unnoticeably,
to the west, over the next house, I remark that the light is perfect. Jay was right, it is a perfect dark purple now, and in its
royal deeps the bundle of eight identically glowing lights is a
mystery and a splendour.

Jay turns to me. "What?"

I've mumbled something and I now realize what.

"You know Pam, right?" I ask, and he nods. "She loved
soccer on TV and used to say the guys looked like gods. At the
end once when they're taking off their shirts and trading them,
and Pam has her eyes hanging out, I said, 'The gods take off
their shirts.' And after that, when something is perfect, really
perfect, it's what we say. A perfect sports car, or prawns in
garlic and butter the waiter puts under your nose, we
announce, 'The gods take off their shirts.'"

"That's pretty good," says Jay.

"We had a few good things."

He says it's great that we had a few good things. We watch
our candle-bag rise and float a little farther away, its speed not
discernable. I voice my worry about it maybe coming down
and landing on a wooden house. In Oregon, I joke. Jay assures
me it won't and I believe him. He turns to me and asks if I
know what *will* happen and I say no. We're standing almost
touching shoulders, and it's as intimate as we've ever been. He
turns to me in this light and his laugh lines and wrinkles are
cut deep. He looks very old, almost instantly, maybe it's the
night, but it's a shocking change in the Jay I know, though I

also understand that my face is doing exactly the same to him.

"What's going to happen," Jay says, "is you're moving in here, you're going to be a big help, I'm going to die, and it's all going to be pretty much okay."

There's no reason in the world to doubt him. In the dark horizon, eight soft lights hang, nestled symmetrically, looking better than science. I believe I'm seeing a thing no one could ever identify or explain.

ACKNOWLEDGEMENTS

Stories in this collection have appeared, in earlier and altered versions, in the following:

"The Kite Trick" in *Granta*; "Honouring Honey" in *Event*, and *Best Canadian Stories*; "The Night Window" in *Malahat Review*, and *Best Canadian Stories*; "The Walk" in *Exile*, and broadcast on CBC's *Between the Covers*; "Forms in Winter" in *Prairie Fire*; "The Beast Waters His Garden of a Summer's Eve" in *Malahat Review*; "Freedom" in *Fiddlehead*; "Work-in-Progress" in *Canadian Fiction Magazine*; "The Green House" in *Fiddlehead*.

ABOUT THE AUTHOR

Bill Gaston is the author of several much-praised story collections and novels, including *Sex is Red*, *The Good Body*, *The Cameraman*, and *Sointula*. He is the recipient of numerous prizes and accolades, including nominations for the Governor General's Literary award (*Gargoyles*), the Giller Prize (*Mount Appetite*), the Ethel Wilson Fiction Prize (*Mount Appetite*, *Sointula*, *Gargoyles*), and the Timothy Findley Award, presented by the Writers' Trust of Canada. Gaston lives with his family in Victoria, British Columbia, where he teaches at the University of Victoria. His next novel, *The Order of Good Cheer*, will be published by House of Anansi in 2008.

Anansi offers complimentary reading guides that can be used with this novel and others.

Ideal for people who love talking about books as much as they love reading them, each reading guide contains in-depth questions about the book that you can use to stimulate interesting discussion at your reading group gathering.

Visit www.anansi.ca to download guides for the following titles:

Gargoyles
Bill Gaston
978-0-88784-776-9 • 0-88784-776-5

The Law of Dreams
Peter Behrens
978-0-88784-774-5 • 0-88784-774-9

The Tracey Fragments
Maureen Medved
978-0-88784-768-4 • 0-88784-768-4

Atonement
Gaétan Soucy
978-0-88784-780-6 • 0-88784-780-3

The Immaculate Conception
Gaétan Soucy
978-0-88784-783-7 • 0-88784-783-8

The Little Girl Who Was Too Fond of Matches
Gaétan Soucy
978-0-88784-781-3 • 0-88784-781-1

Vaudeville!
Gaétan Soucy
978-0-88784-782-0 • 0-88784-782-X

Returning to Earth
Jim Harrison
978-0-88784-786-8 • 0-88784-786-2

True North
Jim Harrison
978-0-88784-729-5 • 0-88784-729-3

Paradise
A. L. Kennedy
978-0-88784-738-7 • 0-88784-738-2

The Big Why
Michael Winter
978-0-88784-734-9 • 0-88784-734-X